Max & Luchia

The Game Makers

by

Kevin Brooke

www.kevinbrooke.com

Max & Luchia
The Game Makers
By
Kevin Brooke

First published in September 2018 by Black Pear Press
www.blackpear.net

ISBN 978-1-910322-75-8

Cover design and illustrations by Seraphim Bryant

Feedback Received From Readers

'I enjoyed Max & Luchia as it led down some unexpected routes'

Ellie Cross, Student at Blessed Edward Oldcorne

'I couldn't put it down. It is an amazing book'

Jake Rouse, Student at Blessed Edward Oldcorne

'I really enjoyed reading about how the children played "Ma-Chia" and always hoped they would get to the next level'

Elinor van Dam, aged 8

'A great adventure, I couldn't put it down. I hope there's another one coming soon!'

Noah Benedict, age 11, Student at Buckland Primary School, Staines, Surrey

For my wife

Feedback Received From Readers   iii

Map Of The Game   161

Acknowledgements   162

Excellent Reviews From Leaders ....

Map Of The Game 101

Acknowledgements 102

My first day at secondary school was exactly as I expected. Everything was strange and confusing.

For a start, Witzengurgle Academy is at least five times bigger than my old school. It has a huge tower that shoots upwards from the main building like a rocket ship. There are four clocks on the tower too, each one faces in a different direction—north, east, south and west.

'Don't you think it looks amazing?' my teacher, Mrs Graham, said.

Me, I'm not sure. I just think it looks a bit odd.

Also, there are three boys called Matt in my class. There's Matt Hummingbird, Matt Parrot and Matt

Bellow. None of them have a round face or dark-coloured hair like me. Even so, at first, everybody seemed to find it difficult to remember who was who. It became so confusing that when Mrs Graham called me Matt instead of Max, I answered, 'Yes, miss.' I'm beginning to think everybody should be called the same name. It would make things a lot easier.

The final bit of 'strange and confusing' was the journey home. When the bell went to signal the end of the day, I headed to the bus stop. I can't read timetables and at our old school, my sister Luchia used to do it for me. So I took a chance and got on the first bus that came along.

I didn't think to question why the man with the yellow-rimmed glasses wasn't the same driver as the one in the morning. It didn't seem to matter. The driver wasn't the only thing that was different. When I looked out of the window, I didn't recognise any of the fields or houses either. With a feeling of panic, I jumped out of my seat and pressed the red button.

'Are you sure you want to get off here?' the driver asked.

I didn't answer and leapt from the bus. Once I was on the pavement, I looked around at the street that was full of unfamiliar things. On my left was a park full of wonky looking trees. On my right was a row of shops with orange-coloured bricks.

I also noticed a bus stop on the other side of the street. It had a sign pointing in the opposite direction to where I'd just come from so I went to cross the road. I know I should have checked both ways, but I didn't. It had started to rain and after pulling my hood down over my face, I stepped forward.

The roar of an engine made me look up to see a flash of black. A car whizzed towards me and I jumped back onto the pavement A high-pitched screech of brakes was followed by a loud crash and a bang.

I stared through the rain to see a black car had crashed into one of the wonky looking trees. Inside the mangled car, a spiky-haired man in a blue jumper was frantically waving his hands through the window.

'Help!' the man shouted. 'Help!'

I was about to run towards him when a woman hobbled out of one of the shops with the orange-

3

coloured bricks. She was wearing a red-and-white-striped apron and had a pink plaster cast on one of her ankles.

'Be careful,' she shouted. 'It could be dangerous.'

I looked at the woman and back at the mangled car, wondering what to do. It didn't take long for me to make up my mind and I raced across the road.

'Push the button next to the handle. Hurry up!' the man in the car shouted.

I squeezed my fingers around the handle and pressed the button as hard as I could.

'It's stuck,' I said, shaking the silver-coloured handle from side to side.

'Try again!'

I pressed the button for a second time. Then I remembered how Mum had tried to open our car sometimes and nudged my knee into the door.

Still nothing.

'Give it a kick!' shouted the spiky-haired man.

I tried to ignore the smell of petrol and the cloud of smoke. I tried to ignore the flames that were flickering across the bonnet. Instead, I kicked the door once, twice, three times.

Finally, it opened and together with the man, I stumbled backwards and collapsed onto the tarmac. The man in the blue jumper was the first to stand up and he grabbed the sleeves of my coat and dragged me towards the pavement. Moments later, the windows in the mangled car made a loud popping sound and the glass shattered into hundreds of sparkling pieces. I lifted my hands to shield my face as the explosion smothered the car in a blanket of flames.

4

And then silence.

It was as though the entire street was recovering from shock. I first realised the world was getting back to normal when the woman in the red-and-white-striped apron hobbled towards me.

'You're a hero!' she shouted. 'You're a hero!'

The spiky-haired man put one hand on my shoulder and shook my hand with the other.

'Thank you,' he said, squeezing so tightly I thought my fingers might break.

'I just wanted to help,' I replied.

Doors to the shops opened. Stunned looking people wandered along the pavement, their eyes focussed on the burning car. I didn't know what to do at first, but then the woman in the apron and the spiky-haired man started to hug and cuddle each other. It was all a bit embarrassing to be honest and so I stepped out of their way.

Moments later, the first of the sirens started to sound. A fire engine arrived, followed by an ambulance and a police car. Suddenly, there were people running in all directions. Firemen carrying long, black hoses, paramedics in green with white boxes under their arms. There were a few police officers too, each of them wearing flat police caps with a black and white check band. Their outstretched arms were interlinked and formed a chain to hold back the onlookers who seemed intent on gaining a closer look at what was left of the car.

Everything I'd done seemed to have been forgotten. This was okay by me, especially as all I wanted to do was find my way home. I walked along the street and hid around a corner. Once I was sure I was on my own, I pressed the button on my watch. I find it difficult to read numbers as well as words and so I waited for the electronic voice. 'The time now is four-fifteen pm, precisely,' it said, to confirm it was definitely time to go home.

The trouble was, in all the confusion, I wasn't sure which side of the street was which.

'You need to cross the road again,' a different voice said, one I didn't recognise.

I turned around. I even went back into the street. Apart from all the people gathered around the burning car, I couldn't see anyone.

'Hello,' I said, but no one replied.

Crossing the road seemed like the right thing to do though and after looking both ways, properly, I went towards the bus stop.

'You need to get on the 919B, not the 919D,' the invisible person said.

Then a red bus came along. It was almost the same colour as the fire engines and it fought its way through the traffic before stopping beside me. I crossed my fingers, showed the driver my bus pass and sat about halfway along the row of seats on the left-hand side.

Fortunately, it turned out to be okay. We've only lived in our new house for three months but as the journey continued, I started to recognise things. The large roundabout at the end of the dual carriageway meant I was about five minutes from home. Soon after, the bus passed the marble soldier who stands guard at the war memorial. This meant it was time to press the button to get off.

WHO GAVE THEIR LIVES
FOR KING AND COUNTRY
IN
THE GREAT WARS
1914-18 ~ 1938-45

When I got home, Mum was waiting by our yellow front door.

'How did it go, Max?' she asked.

'Eventful,' I replied, but nothing else.

I could tell she wanted to ask me more, but I smiled one of my 'everything's okay' smiles and she went into the kitchen. Ever since the divorce and the move, she doesn't seem to have as much time for me and my sister Luchia. In fact, she doesn't seem to have much time for herself either. At one time, her face would have been filled with colourful make-up. Nowadays, her face is as white as flour. I understand because all the changes must have been upsetting for her too.

I took my shoes off and went straight to the room at the back of my house. It's not a big house, particularly in comparison to the one where we used to live. There are three bedrooms upstairs (mine is the smallest), as well as a bathroom. The downstairs is a bit lopsided. At one end is a kitchen you can just about fit in three people if they don't spread out too much. At the other end is a living room and a staircase.

Underneath the staircase is a narrow corridor which leads to a small box room that used to be a garage. To make it my own, I painted each wall in a different colour; red, orange, white and green. Apparently, people have told Mum they think it's artistic. The real reason is that when I found a few tins of paint, there was only a little bit of colour left in each of them.

I looked over at the wooden table in the corner.

8

Next to my computer, was a small, hand-made birthday card. It was written in big capital letters to make sure I could read the words.

"HAPPY ELEVENTH BIRTHDAY MAX!" it said, "LOVE FROM LUCHIA. xx"

She always remembers things, even if she's not very well. She must have waited until Mum was busy, then dodged past her and crept downstairs. After reading the card a few times, I opened the drawer under the table and placed it inside.

There were two reasons for hiding it. One, my birthday was three days ago and two, I didn't want Mum to see it, in case it upset her. Birthdays only happen once a year and I understand how people can forget them. I probably should have said something but I decided not to. Sometimes, it's better not to worry people about certain things. That's what I tell myself anyway.

I jumped onto the orange sofa that's pushed against the wall of the same colour. It's a bit tatty and has a few holes in the cushions. Mum said she wanted to throw it away but I asked her if I could keep it. For some reason, I've always liked it and anyway, it reminds me of the happier times before Mum and Dad started arguing.

Next to the sofa is where I keep my box of multi-coloured building blocks, and after closing the door, I started to build. I hadn't got very far when I had this odd feeling that someone else was in the room. I turned around. I even checked behind the sofa and behind the curtains.

In the end, the odd feeling went away and I carried

on building the castle. It was the one Luchia and I had been talking about recently and I decided I'd take it to her once I'd finished, to cheer her up. It was almost complete, when I heard the same voice as the one I'd heard at the bus stop.

'Close your eyes,' it said.

'Why?' I asked.

For the second time, there was no reply.

I was starting to feel a bit nervous. Mum has always told me not to speak to strangers. Then I remembered how the invisible person had helped me get on the right bus. As I closed my eyes, the room started to spin.

At first, I couldn't see anything, but as the darkness turned to grey and then into white, a few images started to appear. It began with a few clouds floating past me and the occasional patch of blue sky. As the clouds separated I noticed the distinctive shape of a castle below. I began gliding towards it as though I was flying in some sort of dream.

I was almost close enough to land on the top of a castle tower, but then I started to go the other way. I tried to stop myself, force my way down, but no matter what I did, the castle moved further and further into the distance. In the end, it disappeared behind the clouds.

When I opened my eyes, I'd returned to the room at the back of the house.

'Who are you?' I asked.

For the third time, the invisible person didn't reply.

CHAPTER 2

Wednesday morning arrived and Luchia stayed in bed for the fifth day in a row.

'She's got a headache and a sore throat,' Mum said at breakfast.

Luchia's a bit older than I am, but only by eleven months. That's why we're in the same year at school. My birthday is 31st August and so I'm always the youngest. Luchia is usually the oldest. Sometimes people get confused and think that just because we're in the same year we must be twins. Odd really, because even though we've both got chestnut-coloured hair, my eyes are blue and hers are brown.

'Enjoy your day,' Mum said, as I left the house.

With my bag hanging from my shoulder, I headed to the bus stop, the one that's close to the war memorial. As I stood there, I suddenly felt a bit anxious. I wasn't worried about getting the wrong bus this time. Instead, I could sense the invisible person was beside me.

'Have you checked the timetable?' a voice whispered.

I decided to ignore it. Moments later, a bus came along and I stepped on and flashed my bus pass.

'Wrong bus, wrong bus!' the voice said, louder this time. 'You've got on the 919D.'

I looked at the driver and recognised him as the one with the yellow-rimmed glasses. The trouble was, the bus was already moving. I went towards the exit and rang the bell a few times until eventually we came to the next stop. A second red single-decker bus came along soon after. To me, it looked the same as the first one.

'Is this one right?' I asked.

'Yes,' replied the voice. 'This one says 919B on the front.'

I tried to ignore the strange look the driver gave me and walked to a seat about half way along the bus. Ten minutes later, I was in Witzengurgle Street.

The wooden building for the Year 7s is separated from the rest of the school. It has one main classroom with four big square windows that look out onto a car park. It isn't too far away from the main school gates and as we headed towards the wooden hut, I slowed my step and muttered.

'I'm not sure I want to go anymore.'

'It'll be okay, you'll see,' the voice replied.

'Leave me alone, whoever you are.'

12

I get really fed up of people telling me what to do. Especially those who think they know things about you, when they don't.

'Of course,' the voice replied. 'And by the way, my name is Archie.'

Once I was inside the classroom, I sat at the same desk as yesterday at the back. In front of me, groups of girls and boys chatted, smiled, laughed.

Mrs Graham sat behind a large desk at the front. Unlike most schools, in which the Year 7s have different teachers for different subjects, she takes us for almost every lesson. Apart from PE that is. Mr Smart takes us for that.

She's quite a tall lady with dyed red hair, glasses and an upside-down smile. I noticed she was staring at something behind me and I turned to see a white-faced clock. Even though I couldn't read the numbers, I watched the seconds hand tick towards the top.

Mrs Graham stood up.

'Good morning, Year 7,' she said. 'It's time to start the day.'

The others in the class seemed to know exactly what this meant. All around me there was a scraping of chairs across the floor and a gathering of bags and jumpers. I assumed that whatever was happening had probably been explained the previous day and maybe I hadn't been concentrating.

I've been told I do this a lot.

'I need to take the register first,' said Mrs Graham, at which point all the Year 7s sat back down again, apart from me, because I hadn't even moved.

Register complete, Mrs Graham went to the door

of the classroom.

'Tuck your shirts in, blazers on, no fighting, no talking,' she said, and then turned to Matt Hummingbird, 'and NO singing! Okay, single file, follow me.'

The whole class, about thirty of us, followed Mrs Graham in what could almost be described as single file. Across the car park we went and into the main playground. We went past the field with the 'H'-shaped rugby posts at either end and stopped.

'Is everybody here?' Mrs Graham said.

'I'm not,' said Matt Bellow, really loudly.

Mrs Graham ignored him and we carried on. A few more steps and we all trooped to the main building, the one with the odd-looking clock tower. We went through yet another door and pushed our way through a giant green curtain. With Mrs Graham leading us, we headed into a large room with tall windows and sat down on the shiny wooden floor.

I looked behind me and couldn't help but feel a bit daunted by the number of rows there were. I tried to count but there were too many, with each row occupied by bigger and older boys and girls.

'Good morning, Witzengurgle,' said a man on the stage in front of us. He had a ginger beard and narrow eyes.

'As you know, I am the headmaster at this school,' (I didn't actually know this), 'and in the words of the great poet, Witzengurgle himself—nothing is as good as a good start.'

At which point, I switched off completely and all I heard for the next half an hour was a load of "blah,

blah, blah" and some clapping.

Assembly over, we followed Mrs Graham back through the playground, across the car park and into our wooden hut. As before, all of the class chatted amongst themselves except for me.

'Okay, Year 7, it's time for a scavenger hunt,' Mrs Graham said, handing out a sheet of paper to everyone. 'You will see there are seventeen symbols on this page and each symbol relates to something in the school. All you have to do is find them and link the symbols to the items you find. You have until the end of the week to complete the task.'

'The end of the week to complete the task?' Matt Parrot repeated.

'That's right,' Mrs Graham said.

Break time came soon after. Then, after a maths lesson in which I didn't understand a single equation or graph, it was lunchtime. The scavenger hunt I'd been given was particularly good for two reasons. One, it gave me something to do and two, it meant I wouldn't have to stand in the corner of the playground on my own.

'Archie,' I said. 'Are you there?'

'Yes,' he replied.

'Sorry for shouting earlier. Would you be able to help me with this?'

'Of course.'

We made a good team. Whereas he concentrated on the room names and directions, I looked out for the symbols. It was also a great way to get to know my way around, especially as the school is a bit of a maze. Up and down the three sets of stairs in the main building we went and into the sports hall. I even found out there is a swimming pool.

'My goodness,' Mrs Graham said, as I handed back the completed scavenger hunt at the end of the day. 'You've finished this ever so quickly.'

'I was helped by my invisible friend Archie,' I said.

'I'm sure you were,' Mrs Graham replied. She even forced a smile that was the right way up.

On the way home, Archie made sure I caught the right bus.

'How was your day?' Mum asked as I walked through the door at home.

'Eventful,' I replied, for the second day running.

'Anything else, apart from eventful?'

'Just school stuff.'

I went to the back room and pulled out the plastic box full of building blocks.

'Can I help?' Archie asked.

'I thought I'd finish the castle,' I said, clicking the button on my watch to check how much time I had left.

'The time now is four thirty-one pm, precisely,' an electronic voice confirmed. Loads of time. I'd barely even placed one block on top of the other when the room started to spin and I closed my eyes.

When I opened them, I'd travelled to the same place as yesterday. As the clouds separated, I flew towards the castle.

What started as a castle soon grew into something much bigger. Dragons skimmed the tops of the trees as they raced through gaps in the clouds. There was a forest that began at the edge of the beach and then covered the surrounding mountains. At the very top of the highest mountain was a crest of jagged rock that towered over the valleys and streams.

'Would you be able to show me round?' Archie asked as we glided towards the beach.

'What do you mean, show you round?' I replied.

'I thought you might know the best places to go.'

I landed on the wooden drawbridge that led to the stone steps and the castle behind. I hadn't really thought about it when we were flying, but as I stood there I realised Archie wasn't invisible anymore.

He was a bit smaller than me. He was also slightly hunched as though he had a huge weight on his shoulders. He wasn't exactly a man though, not in the normal sense. Even though he had sparkling, hazel-coloured eyes, the rest of him was coloured blue. In fact, he was just like one of the figures I use with my building blocks.

I turned and watched the portcullis rise. It was a sight that was accompanied by the sound of chain scraping against rock as the metal door forced its way up along the grooves.

'Can we go in?' I asked, as we climbed the steps to the castle gate.

'Why not?' Archie replied. 'I've never been inside a castle, have you?'

'Once,' I said, thinking about the time Dad took me, back in the days when people didn't forget my birthday. It's odd, but when we went inside, it looked exactly the same as the one I remembered. The dark colour of the earth was scattered with dirt and gravel and the walls were made up of square-shaped boulders. There were four main towers too, one in each corner with long wooden ledges that ran between the turrets and joined them all together.

'Watch out!' Archie cried, at the sound of hooves clattering up the stone steps into the courtyard. I turned to see a puff of dust and a white horse with a knight sitting on top. He was dressed in a suit of armour that glinted in the sunshine.

The horse reared and I jumped back. I wasn't fast

enough to avoid one of its hooves that struck me on the shoulder and knocked me to the ground. It didn't hurt at first, at least not for a few seconds, but then the pain spread through me.

'On your feet, young peasant,' said the knight through the slot in his visor. 'There's no room for weaklings in this world.'

I stood up, rubbing my shoulder. I was about to reply, when the knight turned, his horse trotting further into the castle. As he rode away, I noticed that his breastplate was facing towards me.

'Archie,' I said. 'Why is his armour on backwards?'

'That's a question for another day,' Archie replied, as a pair of yellow butterflies fluttered past. 'Right now, it's time to go home.'

Moments later, I was standing on the soft carpet in the back room at home. I didn't want to believe it at first, but of course, it was true. The castle, the forest and the mountain had disappeared into the world of faraway imagination.

'Archie, are you still here?' I asked.

'Yes,' he replied.

I turned round and looked for him. Now we were home, however, Archie was invisible again. I pressed the button on my watch to check how long we'd been away.

'The time now is four thirty-one pm, precisely,' the electronic voice said. Exactly the same time as when I'd left the room.

'How is that possible?' I asked.

Archie didn't get the chance to reply because a different and louder voice interrupted our conversation.

'Max, for the third and final time, dinner's ready!' Mum shouted.

I headed towards the kitchen, rubbing my shoulder as I went. Luckily, most of the pain had gone. Even so, I could feel a bruise forming where the horse's hoof had struck.

After I'd finished eating, I ran upstairs to tell Luchia what had happened. I opened her bedroom door to find her sitting up in bed with a thermometer poking out of her mouth. She was leaning forward, her chestnut-coloured hair dangling over her cheeks.

'Headache?' I mouthed.

She nodded and took out the thermometer. 'And a sore throat,' she croaked.

'Max!' Mum shouted from downstairs. 'You know you shouldn't be in there.'

'I'd better go, but I've got lots to tell you,' I said.

Luchia smiled, even though I could tell it was a real effort for her to do so. 'Is it about Archie?'

'You know him as well?'

'Yes,' she said. 'What did you do?'

'When?'

'You must have done something to help someone,' Luchia replied, her brown eyes focussed and alert for the first time since I'd entered the room. 'That's why he's here, as a kind of reward.'

'Come out of there.' It was Mum again and this time she was at the top of the stairs outside Luchia's room.

'I saved someone's life,' I said, as Mum grabbed hold of my arm and pulled me through the doorway.

'You know you shouldn't be going in there, she's still contagious,' she said, closing Luchia's door behind me. 'But thank you for caring. It will mean a lot to her.'

I didn't sleep very well that night. At first, all I could think about was how unwell Luchia looked. As I allowed my mind to drift, my dreams filled with our flight towards the castle. This was followed by the image of the knight with his armour on backwards, as he sat on his big white horse.

I sat up.

'Backwards!' I said, a thought jumping into my head.

Carefully and quietly, I made my way downstairs, along the corridor and into the backroom. I pulled the box from the side of the sofa and delved my hands in amongst the plastic building blocks. Eventually, I found what I was looking for, the figure of a knight, whose breastplate was on back to front.

'Wow,' I said, and took a deep breath.

I headed back upstairs, and then, after the longest night I could ever remember, Thursday morning arrived.

'I'm taking Luchia to see the doctor today,' Mum said. 'She's developed a bit of a rash on her neck and her glands are swollen.'

'Okay,' I replied, and for the third day running, I headed to school on my own. I nearly caught the wrong bus again but thankfully, Archie was there to guide me.

I pushed open the door to the Year 7 building and headed towards the corner of the classroom. As before, Mrs Graham sat at the front, while the others in the class sat in little groups. I turned round, once again mesmerised by the hands on the white-faced clock. Slowly, the second hand ticked its way towards the top, at which point Mrs Graham stood up.

'We have a winner in the scavenger hunt,' she said, scanning the pupils in the classroom as though she was looking for someone. 'Matt, would you come here please.'

The three boys named Matt stood up.

'No, the other one,' Mrs Graham said. 'Is he hiding again?'

Archie gave me a nudge. 'She means you,' he said, 'tell her your real name.'

I pushed myself up from my seat and walked to the front of the classroom.

'I wasn't hiding,' I whispered, as I stood beside her.

'Right, okay,' Mrs Graham replied and turned to the rest of the class. 'I'm sure you'd all like to join me in congratulating Matt on winning the scavenger hunt in double quick time.'

She started to clap, encouraging the pupils to join in. Some of them did and for a little while, I felt quite pleased with myself. I even looked at some of their faces for the first time. As I did so, I noticed something else. One of the boys, the one I knew only as Calum, was glaring at me.

'Well done for completing the hunt,' Mrs Graham said, as I left the classroom at break time. 'It's amazing to think you could finish it so quickly.'

I decided not to mention Archie this time.

'I might not be very good with words and numbers,' I replied. 'But I can see symbols.'

'Oh yes, I remember,' she said. 'Dyslexia is such a trial, isn't it?'

In some ways, I was pleased she didn't go over the top with sympathy like certain others do. For some reason, when I mention dyslexia, people think it's necessary to say, "oh no what a shame" or "oh, I'm terribly sorry". For Mrs Graham to barely say anything was all right by me.

I was thinking about this as I left the classroom and headed to the playground. When I got there, some of the girls were skipping. A few of the boys were leaning against the wire fence that looks out onto the rugby pitch with the 'H'-shaped posts. Some of the others were running around. Everyone had something to do except for me and the boy with dark hair.

He had dark eyes too and he continued to glare at me in the same way as he'd done in the classroom. I looked down towards the tarmac, shuffled into a corner of the playground and twisted my finger through the diamond shapes in the wire. I tried to forget what was happening but for some reason I couldn't. Instead, I kept looking up and every time I did, all I could see were Calum's dark eyes staring back.

CHAPTER 4

The sound of the bell signalled that break time was over. Calum walked across the playground and I followed him, making sure I kept at a safe distance. We were just about to go into the classroom, when he turned and gave me one last stare.

'Come on, you two,' said Mrs Graham, who was standing at the door. 'I can't wait forever.'

Calum sat down in his usual seat about halfway into the classroom and I shuffled to mine. I spent most of the lesson looking at my desk. The last thing I wanted to do was look into those dark eyes of his. I was dreading lunchtime too, and found a table in the corner of the canteen to eat my lunch. I'd nearly finished, when I heard someone start to sing. I turned around to see Calum and the three Matts strolling towards me.

'Don't mind if I sit here do you?' Calum asked, bumping a chair into mine.

I tried not to look, but then a clatter of sweets and chocolate bars fell from his bag onto the table.

'I was supposed to win the scavenger hunt,' he continued, as he chewed one of the bars at the side of his mouth. 'What do you think about that?'

'Sorry,' I replied, hoping he'd get bored and go away.

'It was mine and I was supposed to win. Then you came along and stole it from me.'

'I didn't realise.'

'I didn't realise,' Matt Parrot repeated, sarcastically.

'Well you do now,' Calum said with a smirk as he turned to the others. He pushed a few of the multi-coloured sweets in my direction. 'Do you want one of these?'

'Thank you,' I replied, but when I moved my hand towards the sweets he swiped them away.

'Then buy your own,' he said.

'Then buy your own,' Matt Parrot repeated.

I stayed where I was as Calum and the others stood up. Each of them kicked their feet into my chair leg, jolting me forward in my seat.

'Nice lads,' said Archie, sarcastically, as the four boys walked away. 'What lesson is it next?'

'P.E.'

'That should be okay, shouldn't it?'

'Not really,' I said and headed to the sports hall.

I waited at the changing room door for a few

seconds. Once inside, I noticed a space in one of the corners. I'd only just taken off my jumper, when a bag thumped onto the wooden bench on my left. Another one followed on my right. It was Matt Bellow.

'We're in the gym,' said Calum, talking across me as I faced the wall. 'I've heard it's five-a-side football.'

'Should be fun,' the blonde-haired Matt Bellow shouted out the other side.

I don't particularly like football and hoped Calum was wrong, but of course he wasn't. Even worse, Mr Smart put me in goal.

'Let's see what you can do,' he said.

Not very much as it turned out. I did make a few good saves by the end including a penalty when I dived to my right and pushed the ball over the crossbar. Trouble is, Calum had scored a hat trick by then.

'You'll never get the better of me ever again,' he said, when he picked the ball out of the net for the third time.

I tried not to think about it on the way home. So much so that by the time the bus drove past the soldier at the war memorial, my mind had switched to something else.

'How was your day?' Mum asked as I walked in through the yellow front door.

'Eventful,' I replied.

There's so much I could have said. The thing is, I didn't want to upset her. Anyway, none of this really mattered because I had a plan that would make everything twenty times better.

'Try not to wake your sister,' Mum said, as I made

26

my way up the stairs and towards my room. I waited a moment or two on the landing. Once I heard her go into the kitchen, I tiptoed across the carpet and nudged at Luchia's door.

'Hello,' I whispered.

Luchia turned over. With her head snuggled into her pillow, she peered towards me through a mass of tangled hair.

'How's Witzengurgle?' she said in a croaky voice.

'Just all right,' I said, trying not to look at the rash on the side of her neck. 'Anyway, I'm going to try something, so get ready okay?'

Luchia smiled, weakly, but it was definitely a smile.

Suddenly, there was the clatter of feet racing up the stairs. 'I told you not to disturb her,' Mum said, grabbing my arm, her fingernails pinching into my skin as she dragged me into my room. 'She needs rest, Max, don't you understand?'

'Sorry.'

I closed the door and waited a few seconds for Mum to go back downstairs.

'Archie,' I said. 'Are you there?'

'I'm always here when you need me.'

'Thank you.'

After tea, I headed into the back room. I pulled the box of building blocks from beside the sofa and started to build. The narrow, angled bottom of a ship came first. I added a hull at the front and a rudder at the back. A port side, a starboard side followed and then the deck of the ship sprouted a tall thin mast with sails stretching left and right.

'Are you ready?' Archie asked.

'Yes,' I replied, as the room started to spin. As it began to darken, I closed my eyes. When I opened them, Archie and I were standing on opposite sides of the ship I'd just built. We'd only been there for a moment, when it started to tilt and sway. Occasionally, one of the bigger waves leapt over the side.

'Storm approaching,' Archie shouted.

I looked up to see a mass of clouds heading in our direction, their ragged shapes connecting and gathering into one huge, menacing sprawl of darkness. A fork of lightning ripped through the gloom. A clap of thunder shook the deck beneath my feet and it started to rain. With raindrops the size of golf balls crashing onto the deck, I protected my face with my hands and scrambled across to Archie.

'We need to lower the sails,' I said.

'Aye, aye, Captain,' Archie replied.

As the rain continued to fall, we each grabbed a bucket. The trouble was, with each bucketful of water we threw over the side, five were thrown back by the waves as the ship rocked up and down.

'I'm sorry, Max, but I need to take us back,' said Archie. 'I don't think it's safe anymore.'

I could tell he was scared but I was determined to keep going for as long as possible. Moments later, yet another huge wave leapt over the edge of the ship and smashed its way onto the deck. Another jagged fork of lightning ripped the sky in two. It was soon followed by a second, angry bellow of thunder.

'Don't worry,' I said. 'We'll be okay.'

'But, Max, I've lost control,' Archie said. 'It's too dangerous.'

I stared into the distance, doing my best to think about a calm and sunny day. Nothing happened at first so I tried again, this time closing my eyes and concentrating as hard as I could. I imagined a row of seashells on the beach, a crystal blue sky and the sunshine glistening on the ripples in the sea below.

When I opened my eyes, a few of the clouds had

separated. A golden beam of light forced its way through one of the gaps and rested on the surface of the water. As the storm continued to lose its power, a kaleidoscope of colour rose from the sea and circled around us.

'Rainbow,' I said. 'I told you we'd be okay.'

Almost as blue as the sky behind him, Archie came towards me. 'That shouldn't happen, Max, I'm sorry. I shouldn't be able to lose control like that.'

'There's something else,' I said, trying not to laugh. 'Something that's even more amazing.'

'We need to untie the sails and put them back up,' said a voice behind me, the voice of a young girl with brown eyes and chestnut-coloured, shoulder-length hair.

'Aye, aye, skipper,' Archie said, then looked to his left. 'Luchia, how did you get here?'

'Max asked me,' she replied.

'But that shouldn't happen either,' said Archie.

'Oh,' I said, pointing at the island in front of us. 'You might recognise this place as well.'

I suppose I should have warned him really, but I wanted to see his reaction.

On the island, there were hills and mountains. At the top of the very highest mountain was a crest of jagged rock that towered over valleys and streams. Dragons raced through clouds that floated above the towers of a castle. I looked towards the beach, where a knight was sitting on top of a white horse.

'What do you think, Archie?' I asked, but as I glanced towards him, I noticed that he'd started to wobble. It was as though, all of a sudden, he'd lost the

30

power in his legs.

Moments later, they collapsed beneath him and he fell into a heap.

CHAPTER 5

'What do we do now?' I asked.

Luchia giggled as she knelt beside Archie. 'I might try this,' she said, waving her hands across his face in a kind of fanning motion.

Eventually, Archie stirred, opened his eyes and sat up. 'Where am I?'

'On the boat, heading for the island,' I replied.

'Oh yes, I remember,' he said, rubbing his hazel-coloured eyes and looking at each of us in turn.

'You want to know how I got here, don't you?' Luchia asked. 'Like I said before, Max asked me if I wanted to join in, so I did.'

'I kind of imagined she was with us,' I added, 'and there she was.'

'Right,' Archie said. 'This shouldn't happen though, it really shouldn't. I'm the one who's supposed to be in control.'

'Sorry,' I said.

'Next time,' said Archie. 'It would be great if you could let me know what you're doing.'

'There is one other thing,' I said.

'Go on.'

'It also means we've started the game.'

'What game?'

'Our game,' said Luchia. 'We call it Ma-Chia.'

'It's a kind of mishmash of our names,' I added.

'I think you'd better explain this to me another time,' said Archie, as a small, yellow butterfly landed on the ship's deck beside us. 'Right now, it's time we all went home.'

Within moments, I was back in the room in which we'd started. I pressed the button on my watch to make sure. 'The time now is six fifty-three pm, precisely,' the voice said. As before, we'd come home at exactly the same time as when we'd left. I heard some footsteps in the small corridor outside the room and I pushed the box of building blocks to one side.

It was Mum.

'The doctor thinks Luchia has scarlet fever,' she said. She walked towards me and placed the palm of her hand against my forehead. 'At least you seem all right.'

'I'm fine,' I replied, 'and Luchia seemed fine too when we were on the ship.'

'What ship?' she asked.

I was about to tell her everything. I was tempted to

tell her about the storm, the island and the castle but changed my mind.

'Oh, just a game we're playing,' I said.

'You be careful about involving Luchia. The doctor said she needs time to recuperate.'

'Okay.'

'One more thing,' Mum said. 'Happy Birthday for Saturday.'

She handed me a card and a small box that was tied with a bow. I opened the card straight away and found a ten-pound note.

'Thank you,' I replied. I wish I could have thought of something better to say. I know how guilty she would have felt when she'd realised she'd forgotten.

I opened the box to find two cupcakes. One had blue icing and the other one orange. In the middle of each of them was a single candle.

'I'm so sorry I didn't remember your special day,' she said, as she pulled me towards her and gave me a hug. 'Things will get back to normal soon, I promise.'

The next morning, I headed off to school on my own once more. At least I was getting to know the buses. I was even tempted to pretend to get on the wrong one, just to see how Archie would react, but decided not to.

I hadn't been in the classroom long, when Mrs Graham stood up.

'I'll be back in a minute,' she said.

She'd only been gone a few moments when some of the boys started running around and smashing into desks. Matt Hummingbird and some of the girls were singing or at least, I think they were singing.

I tried to ignore them and concentrated on the piece of writing that Mrs Graham had given us all to read. It was a newspaper article from the Witzengurgle Gazette. I was using my shaded blue window ruler, the one with the blue line across the middle to stop the words from jumping around the page. It's another reason I like to sit at the back in the corner. It means that no one asks me embarrassing questions.

I was about halfway down the page when I realised I knew the story. It was about an accident that happened recently. At the top of the article was a heading:

"Hero Revealed: Boy From Witzengurgle Academy Saves Man's Life."

Everyone in the class had been given a copy of the paper but no one else seemed to be reading it. No one that is, except me. Most of the copies were lying on the floor. One or two of them were lying on desks. Some of the others were whizzing through the air in the shape of paper aeroplanes.

The classroom door opened, at which point everyone ran back to their seats. It was Mrs Graham and the woman who'd hobbled out of the shops with the orange-coloured bricks. She wasn't wearing the red-and-white striped apron anymore. She didn't have the pink plaster cast on her ankle either, but I could tell it was her.

'I hope you've all read the newspaper article because here he is, the hero of the hour,' Mrs Graham said.

'You should be proud of yourself,' Archie whispered. 'It's about time you received some recognition.'

'It's not like that,' I said. 'Didn't you read the article?'

I shouldn't have snapped at him, but I couldn't help it. Mrs Graham hadn't been the only person to have left the room ten minutes before.

'Come on then, stand up,' Mrs Graham said and the rest of the class did so. I probably should have done so too, but I didn't. Instead, I looked towards the front of the class where Mrs Graham and the woman without her apron were standing. Beside them, in all his smiling smugness, was Calum.

'I think our hero deserves a round of applause, don't you?'

Some of the others in the class started to clap and a few more joined in. I looked down at my desk and read a few more words of the article:

Ignoring smoke, flames and the threat of danger Calum, aged 11, forced the door of the black Volvo Estate open, moments before it exploded into a ball of flames.
'He was amazing, a real hero,' an onlooker at the scene of the accident said.
'I had to do something,' the young man, Calum, confirmed.

The article went on to explain how Calum had answered an appeal for witnesses. It mentioned his reluctance to come forward but how, as an example to others, he'd decided it "was the best thing to do".

'Tell her the truth,' Archie said. 'Mrs Graham needs

to know it was you.'

'It's too late,' I said, remembering Calum's words about how I'd never get the better of him again. 'Anyway, that woman with Mrs Graham obviously thinks it was him.'

'We need to find the man with the spiky hair,' Archie said, but I wasn't really interested anymore.

I allowed the rest of the day to drift past. I spent most of it trying not to listen to Calum as he boasted to anyone he could find about how brave he'd been. Whether he knew it had been me who'd saved the man, I don't know. Then again, I'm not sure he would have actually cared.

'How was your day?' Mum asked, as I walked into the house.

'Eventful,' I replied.

'At least you have the weekend to relax,' she said.

I went upstairs and stood on the landing. When I thought it was safe, I leant over and placed my head against Luchia's bedroom door.

'You know what will happen if your mum finds you in there, don't you?' Archie said.

'Yes,' I said, pushing the door open. 'But I really need to speak to Luchia.'

As always, the curtains were drawn and the room was full of shadows.

'Hello, Max,' she said in a whisper.

'Mum told me you saw the doctor again,' I said, stepping towards her bed. 'She said it might be scarlet fever.'

She rolled over to face me. 'I've been given some

antibiotics,' she replied, scratching at the sunburn-coloured rash on her cheek. 'Everywhere is so itchy.'

I couldn't help but feel disappointed. Not only for her, but also because of what Mum had said about Luchia needing to rest. I know it's a bit selfish but I couldn't help it.

'I suppose we can wait for a while before we go back to the island,' I said.

She sat up. 'Whatever happens, I need to carry on. Please, Max, please!'

'But Mum says I shouldn't involve you.'

'Surely you haven't told her.'

I shook my head. 'I just said we were playing a game.'

'We will tell her everything one day,' Luchia said. 'Not yet please, because when we were on that ship, I felt better than I have done for ages.'

I smiled. 'Maybe we should make things a bit more interesting.'

'You mean?'

'Yes I do. It's about time we started Ma-Chia at Level 1.'

Archie had been quiet so far, but not anymore. 'Is anyone going to let me into this little secret?' he asked.

'I'll let Max tell you,' Luchia said.

'See you in a while,' I said and closed the door behind me. I carefully made my way down the stairs, past the living room and along the narrow hallway. When I reached the back room, I pulled the plastic box that contained the ship and the castle towards me. Instead of adding to the ship, I concentrated on a small rowing boat that included a pair of oars with flat spoons at one end.

'We really need your help,' I said to Archie. 'I know I've barely spoken to you all day, but I really need you to help us find some things in our game.'

'Like a scavenger hunt.'

'Something like that.'

'You will tell me what's going on soon, won't you?' he asked.

'Of course,' I said, as the room began to spin.

'Cast anchor!' Luchia shouted, her chestnut hair tied into a ponytail.

With a rattle of metal and a splash, the anchor dived from the ship and through the surface of the sea.

'Lower the landing boat!' I said, as I grabbed at Archie's arm. 'Come on, or we'll miss it.'

He followed me over the side of the ship and into the small wooden boat I'd just built in the back room. Archie and I sat on a wooden plank in the middle and lifted our oars so that they pointed upwards. With a screech of gears, Luchia turned the handle on the winch to lower us down to the water. The boat bobbed on the waves at first, but settled down when

Luchia sat down at the front.

'After three,' I said, placing my oar through the rowlock on the side of the boat and lowering it into the sea. 'One, two, three and row.'

'Steady!' cried Luchia, and for a moment I was convinced she was talking to me. 'Archie, please copy Max or we'll go around in circles.'

'Heave,' I shouted. 'Heave.'

After a while, we started to move in the right direction towards the island that was soon only a few metres away. I looked up to see the knight standing on the beach.

He held the reins of the white horse in one hand. His other hand reached towards us.

'Welcome, young peasant,' the voice of the knight echoed through the letterbox-shaped opening in his visor as the front of our boat carved a 'V' shape into the sand. 'I see you've brought some friends. Let's hope they have more courage than you.'

'Did you know your breastplate is on backwards?' I asked.

'Is it?' he replied, lifting a red book from underneath his armour that said, "How To Be A Knight" on the outside. He then compared the drawing on the front page with himself. 'Oh yes, I see what you mean.'

Once we'd all managed to get out of the boat, the three of us lined up alongside one another on the beach.

In front of us was the knight. The visor on his helmet was fully open now revealing his face and a wispy beard in a single line that hung from his chin.

'Welcome to you all,' he said, 'and congratulations on reaching the island. It is now time to commence Ma-Chia at Level 1.'

'Oh, so you know about this game as well do you?' Archie said. 'I'm glad someone does.'

The knight ignored him and handed each of us a small, plastic device that was no bigger than the palm of my hand. In the middle was a narrow screen.

'These are your life monitors,' he said. 'You must pay attention to them at all times.'

'What do they do?' asked Archie.

'Good question,' replied the knight. 'They will inform you if you need to gain energy. This can be achieved by locating ration packs marked with an

42

apple that will also be filled with useful implements. Remember to leave the ones with the image of skull and crossbones as these will do you harm. The rest of the time, you will be avoiding the monsters in the forest.'

'I'm sorry,' Archie said, 'did you say monsters?'

'That's right,' the knight replied, 'monsters that will attack you, but don't worry, there are plenty of ways you can look after yourself.'

Luchia took hold of Archie's hand. 'Don't worry, we'll protect you.'

'At the end of each level,' said the knight, as he placed his foot into the stirrup and mounted his horse, 'you will get the chance to take the life monitors home to recharge them. Be careful not to show them to anyone else as this will have severe consequences.'

'Recharge them?' Archie asked.

'That's what it says here,' the knight replied, lifting a second book from his armour. It was a blue book that said, "CODE OF CONDUCT"' on the outside.

'Yes, you know, like an iPod or something,' Luchia said.

'I'm sorry, like a what?' Archie replied. 'I might know little bits about your world, but not everything.'

'Don't worry,' I said. 'We'll show you.'

'I wish you great fortune!' said the knight, this time looking directly at me. 'Learn to be chivalrous, young man, and before you know it, you will be a hero.'

The knight set off, his horse leaving a trail of hoof prints in the sand. As he did so, I thought about what he'd said. The word hero seemed like a strange word to use for a game and it made me think about what

43

happened in the classroom. I thought about how Calum had been called a hero, when all he'd done was steal the credit for something I'd done.

I was beginning to wonder whether a similar thing might happen again but then I looked at Luchia. Her eyes were so full of excitement, I realised that no matter what happened, it was going to be worth it.

Archie, on the other hand, appeared to be worried about something else. 'It is only a game, isn't it?' he asked.

'Most of the time,' I replied.

'Have you switched on your life monitors?' Luchia asked. 'You won't be allowed into the forest if you haven't.'

I pulled the device from my pocket. On one of the sides was a black plastic button and I pressed it. Immediately, a green light flashed a row of five bars across the screen.

'That's our energy source,' I told Archie, pressing the button on his monitor as well. 'Just don't let it go to red.'

We walked into the forest and followed a single path that led us through the trees. Once we'd gone a few steps, Luchia went one way and I went the other. I ran into the overhanging branches and soon found a small, square parcel with an apple on one side.

'Got one!' I shouted.

I opened it up to find a pair of orange glow sticks and so headed back to the path where Luchia was holding three rucksacks.

'One each,' she said.

I put the glow sticks into my rucksack. 'Let's see

what else we can find.'

Archie, meanwhile, seemed oblivious to what we were doing and continued to stroll along the path.

'Do we need to head for those caves over there?' he asked, pointing towards the dark holes in the side of a hill on our right.

I stopped where I was. 'Luchia, have you seen the caves?'

Luchia came alongside me. 'We need to be ready.'

'For what?' asked Archie.

'For Level 2,' I replied. 'If we get through Level 1, we head into the caves. Don't you know anything?'

'No, because no one has told me.'

'Jester!' Luchia shouted.

I turned.

Behind me was a man with a floppy hat, a red smiling mouth and a multi-coloured harlequin suit. He was jumping up and down and bounding from place to place. For a moment, I was certain he was taunting me by mimicking the way words jump around the page when I read. Then I looked closer to see that his suit was covered in letters and numbers.

The jester leapt in our direction and I ran into the trees as quickly as I could. When I looked back, I realised Archie hadn't moved. Instead, he stood in the middle of the path, open-mouthed as a different jester moved towards him. She had a diamond pattern on her leggings and a hat that was weighed down with bells.

Moments later, there was a puff of smoke as Archie was propelled high into the sky as though he'd been fired from a cannon. Higher, higher he went, above the tops of the trees before tumbling onto the ground.

I ran towards him.

'Are you okay?' I asked.

'A bit winded,' he replied, brushing some of the mud from his arm.

I sat beside him, as the green colour in his face returned to blue. 'You'll be okay in a minute.'

'What was that?'

'Jester,' I said. 'You need to watch out for them. You need to be on your guard.'

'I thought jesters were supposed to be funny.'

'Not these ones,' I replied.

Luchia crawled towards us. 'Has everyone got their life monitor?' she asked, showing us the screen on hers that had five bars of green.

I retrieved mine from my pocket to see that I had four and a half bars.

Archie did the same. A thin line of red.

'What does that mean?' he asked.

'Game over,' I said, as a pair of yellow butterflies fluttered past to confirm we were going home.

CHAPTER 7

Game over meant Luchia going back to bed with a
sore throat and her annoying rash. It also left me with
the dread of going back to school. I could already
imagine sitting at the back of the class with no one to
talk to. I could also picture the hostile eyes of Calum.

All thanks to Archie.

'What does game over mean?' he asked. 'Do we get
another go?'

I didn't reply because I didn't want to hurt his
feelings and so tried to say something without
speaking. I lifted up the ship I'd built and stared at it
from end to end. I then put it back on the floor and
started to dismantle it, piece by piece.

Afterwards, I went upstairs to see Luchia. I

deliberately made some heavy footsteps across the landing towards my room. After tiptoeing back the other way, I pushed open the door to find that Luchia was facing away from the door.

'Are you okay, Max?' she asked.

'Not really.'

Neither of us said anything for a while, but then Luchia turned to face me. 'You never know, there might be a way to get us back in.'

'I hope so,' I said.

'Maybe I can help,' Archie suggested.

I couldn't resist any longer. 'No you can't because you've ruined everything. You should have been collecting ration packs when we were in the forest. You should have run when we did.'

'I didn't know, I'm sorry,' Archie replied.

'Didn't you listen to the knight?' I said.

'It's not Archie's fault,' said Luchia. 'It's ours. We should have explained things properly before we started.'

'But how would he understand?' I asked. 'He doesn't even know what an iPod is.'

'You could always try, Max,' Luchia said. 'I know it's been difficult for you since Mum and Dad split up.'

'What's that got to do with anything?'

'I didn't want to say it, but ever since it happened, you've stopped telling people things.'

'No I haven't.'

'Sorry, Max, but it's true,' Luchia said. 'So please just remember, Archie needs help from us just like we need help from him.'

I was really annoyed at first. Who was she to tell

me what to do and then blame it all on Dad? I didn't say anything though, not for a while, and when I did look up, she gave me one of her 'you know I'm right' looks.

I took a deep breath. 'Sorry, Archie,' I said. 'It's just really disappointing.'

'For me too,' Archie replied. 'But surely we can get back into the game somehow.'

'We can get back to the island,' said Luchia. 'But until the knight gives us another chance, we can't go into the forest.'

I got the impression Luchia was even more disappointed than I was. From what she'd said, I could also tell that her disappointment wasn't only aimed at Archie.

'Show him the book, Max,' she said, 'and don't forget to plug in your life monitors.'

I picked up the purple-coloured book from her bedside table and headed down the stairs. After collecting a glass of water from the kitchen I went into the back room.

'Archie, are you there?' I asked, and opened the purple book that said 'Ma-Chia' on the outside and allowed him to see the drawings on the pages inside.

'This is the ship you made,' he said, 'and this one's the castle.'

'That's right, and this is the knight we met, along with his white horse,' I replied. 'Until now, all we had was my drawings and Luchia's words. Then you came along and made it all come true.'

Just as it had been in Luchia's room, there was silence as though neither of us knew what to say.

50

'I can understand now why you were able to take control on the ship,' said Archie, 'and how you were able to invite Luchia.'

'It's her game as much as it is mine,' I said.

Archie went quiet for a moment or two, but then spoke once again. 'But if it's your game, I still don't understand why you can't let yourselves back in.'

'We can't just change the rules,' I replied. 'Otherwise it wouldn't be a game would it? All we've done is make a few suggestions about how it should be set up and the game kind of expands itself.'

'Like an imagination,' said Archie.

'I suppose so.'

'Can you leave the book open at this page for me?' he asked. 'I'd like to memorise the details a bit, in case we get another chance.'

The rest of the weekend came and went without much happening. After plugging our life monitors into my computer, I spent most of the time in the back room building things. Archie, meanwhile, would occasionally ask me to turn the pages in the rulebook.

On Sunday, when it was quiet, I crept into Luchia's room. She was asleep, so I left one of my birthday cakes on her bedside table.

As always, Monday arrived all too quickly and

once again, I was struggling to concentrate during the first lesson of the week, which was English.

'Matt, are you listening?' Mrs Graham shouted more times than I could count.

'Yes, miss,' I said, and every time I did so, Calum turned around and stared at me with those dark eyes of his.

'Don't let him get to you,' Archie said. 'Don't let his problem become your problem.'

It was easy for him to say. He wasn't the one being glared at.

The bell sounded for break time and I headed to my corner in the playground. I looped my fingers through the diamond shapes in the wire and stared at the 'H'-shaped posts in the rugby field. After a while, I heard the sound of singing and I turned to see Matt Hummingbird standing beside Calum. The other two Matts were there as well, along with a few other boys from class.

'What do you want?' I asked.

Calum laughed.

'Max, Max, Max,' he said, as he stepped forward, slowly and deliberately. He turned to the others and encouraged them to join in. As always, Matt Bellow was particularly loud and before I'd had the chance to move, I was surrounded.

'Do something, Archie, please,' I said.

'I wish I could,' he replied. 'But Calum isn't alone.'

It was such an odd thing to say. I knew Calum wasn't alone because I could see at least six of them, maybe seven.

'Anuska's with him,' Archie said, and then in a

52

whisper. 'How did Calum manage to get himself a guiding spirit?'

'Who's Anuska?' I asked, but before I'd finished the question, I could sense that Archie had gone.

'Max, Max, Max,' the group continued to chant.

Calum took a step back and waved his arms as though he was conducting an orchestra. At the same time, he was continuing to look at me with one of his nasty, self-satisfied expressions that hardened into a snarl.

I closed my eyes and tried to imagine I was somewhere else. I tried to picture myself back on the deck of the ship, on the island and amongst the trees in the forest but it didn't work. No matter how much I tried to think of other things, I couldn't get the vision of Calum's taunting face out of my mind.

Then the image of his face changed into something far worse. It was a person, or at least it was a kind of a person because instead of walking, she appeared to

slither. With long, blonde hair, she was dressed in grey and a black-coloured veil covered part of her face. Above the veil was a set of penetrating green eyes.

I started to shake. Not from fear but from a cold wind that crept underneath my shirt. I clasped my arms around my chest in an effort to keep warm. Moments later, the screech of the bell signalled the end of break time and the cold wind released itself.

I opened my eyes to see that Calum was standing, sneering, his top lip raised to allow me a glimpse of his teeth.

'See you in class,' he said, then turned and followed the others.

As he walked away, I could sense that Archie had returned. 'I'm sorry for leaving you. A spirit called Anuska pushed me away.'

'I think I saw her,' I replied. 'Who is she?'

Archie paused. 'Remember how Calum told you that you'll never get the better of him ever again?'

'After football?'

'Anuska said the same thing to me once,' said Archie, 'but how did you see her? You shouldn't be able to do that.'

'All I did was close my eyes and she appeared,' I replied.

'That's the power of your imagination I think,' said Archie, 'letting the bad things in as well as the good.'

'Will she come back? Will I see her every time I close my eyes?'

'Only occasionally,' he said. 'It will have taken a lot of her strength to enter your mind.'

'Can you do things like that? Enter people's minds I mean.'

'Sometimes,' Archie replied. 'Sometimes.'

CHAPTER 8

Mrs Graham started the next lesson. I've always liked Roman History and it was just what I needed to take my mind off what happened in the playground.

She pointed to a map on the wall behind her. 'Does anyone know anything about Roman roads?' she asked.

For once, I knew the answer and lifted my hand.

'They were straight!' I said.

'Was that you, Matt?' Mrs Graham replied, looking in my direction.

As she stepped towards me, her appearance changed. The colour of her eyes changed to a penetrating green and her dyed red hair altered to blonde. The closer she came, the more her movement appeared to fall into a slither as a cold wind brushed at my chest.

'Leave me alone!' I shouted, burying my head in my hands.

When I looked up, Mrs Graham had returned to the teacher I recognised.

'Are you okay, Matt?' she asked.

'Fine,' I replied.

'You're shaking. Are you sure you're all right?'

'Yes, I must be imagining things.'

Mrs Graham waited for a moment. She then turned, went to the front of the classroom and carried on with the lesson.

'Archie,' I whispered.

No answer.

'Archie,' I said. 'Where are you?'

'I'm here, Max,' he said, eventually. 'But why did Anuska have to be a snake? I hate snakes!'

'She's scary.'

'I know,' said Archie. 'I'll try not to leave you again.'

He was great, I have to say. Every time Anuska pushed her slithering image into my mind, Archie helped me to force her away. Every time I felt a cold wind, he'd speak to me and make me think about warm days in the sunshine.

Finally, thankfully, it was time to go home.

'I need to visit somebody,' Archie said, once he'd made sure I'd caught the right bus. 'I'll be back soon.'

He only seemed to leave me for a minute, maybe two, until I could sense he'd returned.

'I've managed to arrange something,' he said. 'As of

56

tonight, we are back in the game.'

'How?'

'I spoke to the knight,' said Archie. 'I told him it was all my fault it ended last time and pleaded for another go.'

'And he agreed?'

'He did mention something about conditions,' Archie said. 'I told him we'd be happy to accept anything as long as he gives us another chance. '

'How was your day?' Mum asked, as I walked in through the door.

'Eventful,' I said.

'One of these days,' she replied, 'you're going to have to tell me what you mean by that word of yours.'

'Of course,' I said, 'just not today if that's all right.'

After taking my shoes off, I ran upstairs and crept into Luchia's room. 'Are you awake?'

Even though the curtains were drawn, I could see she was sitting up.

'Archie's managed to get us back in the game,' I said, 'so I thought I'd give him another chance. What do you think?'

Luchia looked back at me. 'As long as he's ready.'

'Are you ready, Archie?' I asked.

'Yes,' he replied. 'I think so.'

'All right,' I said. 'Let's do it!'

I tiptoed out of the room and headed back downstairs.

'Is there anything you want to tell me, Max?' Mum asked, standing at the kitchen door. 'You look a bit anxious.'

'Everything's fine, I promise,' I said. She was wearing one of those expressions she has sometimes, the ones that tell me I'm in for a bit of a grilling.

'You need to say if there's anything wrong,' she replied.

I wasn't in the mood for it though. It's all right for Luchia to tell me I've been quiet since Dad left, but she's not the one that Mum takes her anger out on. So I changed the subject. 'What's for tea?'

'Sausage and chips, so don't go too far will you.'

'No,' I replied, smiling and turned away.

I then headed to the back room and, thinking about the next level of the game, I built a small mound of blocks with a mouth-shaped opening on one side. As the room began to spin, I grabbed our life monitors and closed my eyes. When I opened them, I was back on the main path in the middle of the forest.

'Welcome, peasants,' said the knight, standing in front of us. 'For Level 2, you will be required to demonstrate considerable foolhardiness.'

'Level 2?' Luchia asked.

'After speaking with Archie,' the knight said, with a smile, 'it has been decided that to save time, and because I like you, you have been upgraded.'

'Oh,' Luchia said. 'Thank you.'

'Don't thank me yet,' the knight said. 'To progress, you will also be required to conquer aspects of Level 1.'

'Does that mean we're doing both Levels in one go?' I asked.

'That is indeed correct,' said the knight. 'Sounds like fun eh?'

He turned, as though he was about to walk away but then stopped.

'One question,' he said. 'I've been told you might find some interesting items in these treasure packs of yours. If anyone finds a round table, you will let me know won't you?'

'A round table,' said Archie. 'Is that likely?'

'No idea,' he replied, lifting the "How To Be A Knight" book from his armour. 'I just think I should have one.'

Archie looked at me.

I shrugged, so he looked at Luchia who was hiding her face behind her hand, as though she was trying not to laugh.

'Oh, and to make things easier,' the knight continued, 'I've been thinking about a name for my horse.'

'That's nice,' said Archie. 'Any ideas?'

'Galahad,' the knight replied, reading from the 'How to be a Knight' book once more. 'One who is gallant and pure. It seems perfect, don't you think?'

'Why not?' Archie said

'And don't forget to search for round tables,' said the knight, as his silver armour disappeared among the branches of the pine trees.

'How strange,' said Archie.

'I think we should get on with the game,' Luchia said, amidst giggles. 'Come on, it's time we went into the caves.'

'Maybe we'll find a table in there,' I suggested, but as I looked over at the opening, I didn't feel like making jokes anymore.

Above the cave, was a pair of black, soulless eyes. In the centre of the entrance were two 'V'-shaped stones that hung from the roof like fangs. Behind the fangs was a mouth-shaped entrance of darkness.

'Has anyone got anything useful?' Luchia asked.

'Is this any good,' I said, lifting an orange glow stick from my rucksack.

I was at the front and Archie at the back. With the sound of crunching stones beneath our feet we edged our way forward into the gloom.

'Sshhh!' said Luchia, as though it was my fault we were making a noise.

Using the glow stick to light our path, we started to speed up. After a few minutes, we reached a fork in the cave giving us the choice of two tunnels. One of them headed upwards and the other one down.

'Which way?' Luchia asked.

'Down,' I suggested, not really knowing why.

We hadn't gone far when we stopped. I think it was because we were all mesmerised by the swishing sound of waves that echoed around us.

'We should go up, really quickly,' I said.

Even in the gloom, I could see the glimmer of white and a pair of bright green eyes belonging to the seaspirits that were racing in our direction. We dashed along the tunnel as fast as we could. The further we went, however, the narrower it became as the ceiling lowered and the stone walls closed in on both sides. We rounded a corner only to find that we'd reached a dead end.

'Now what?' said Archie.

I looked back along the tunnel. There wasn't just

one spirit chasing us now, but three of them, their sting-filled tentacles hanging like ribbons below their cloud-like bodies.

As they came closer, I could hear their whispering voices. 'Capture them...bring them with us...into the deep.'

'Use these,' Luchia replied, handing me a narrow brown stick and some matches.

'Dynamite!' said Archie. 'You can't use that in here.'

'We haven't got much choice,' I said, placing the stick on a small ledge on the wall. 'Stand back!'

With my hands over my ears, I watched the wick fizz and spark and then I headed back round the corner. I crouched as low as I could and waited. Seconds later, a wall trembling, ear-blasting explosion echoed around us. Once the ground had stopped shaking, I looked up. At first, all I could see was a thick cloud of dust and smoke but as it began to disperse, I noticed a large gap in the wall.

'Come on!' I shouted.

We'd only just made it through the gap when the ceiling collapsed into a pile of rubble, trapping the seaspirits on the other side.

'That was close,' Archie said.

'That was too close,' I agreed.

Luchia was standing, staring. 'We need to keep going,' she said.

In front of her, or should I say above her, was a chainmail-covered, oily black body attached to the ceiling. Part-man, part-vampire, its bulging eyes stared directly at me as its wings lowered, opened and prepared for flight.

'Have you got anything else, Max?' asked Archie.

I checked my rucksack. 'Nothing useful.'

As the dust continued to clear, I noticed it wasn't

just one set of wings that was opening, but many, many more. There was something else too. The vampire berserkers were carrying swords.

'I think we should go,' Archie said.

'Really?' I said, sarcastically.

'My turn,' said Luchia, grabbing the glow stick from me.

She's fast my sister, really fast and probably quick enough to outrun a seaspirit or two. Nimble-bodied, wide-winged vampires, however, they're something else.

In the distance, a small circle of light guided us towards the exit of the tunnel.

'We're nearly there!' Archie shouted.

It didn't feel like that to me and the further we went, the louder the hiss and the bloodthirsty scream of the berserkers became.

'Catch them.'

'Chop them.'

'Feast on them.'

One was so close, I could feel his breath on the back of my neck until, finally, we raced through the mouth-shaped opening.

The vampires followed us out, their swords clattering against the fang-shaped stones that hung from the ceiling of the tunnel. I turned around, just in time to see their chainmail-covered bodies explode into flames at their exposure to daylight. With a clatter of metal, the swords they'd been carrying dropped onto the ground beside us.

'Grab one!' said Luchia.

I did as she said and then looked up to see a jester bounding through the trees. With one giant leap, the multi-coloured, smiling assassin threw himself in my direction.

CHAPTER 9

I swung my sword, the jester's harlequin suit shattering into a cloud of colourful, diamond-shaped pieces that sprinkled onto the ground.

'Watch out!' shouted Luchia.

I turned to see nine, maybe ten jesters racing through the trees. Archie, Luchia and I stepped forward, our swords flashing in the sunlight.

But then one of them changed direction.

'On your right,' Archie shouted

'Behind you!' said Luchia.

I swivelled and hit him moments before he exploded on the ground. Another jester down and yet still they jumped towards us from every angle. I was certain we'd be overrun but every time one of them bounded out of the forest, one of us was ready with a swirl of a sword.

'Keep going,' I shouted until, finally, every single jester was nothing more than a heap of colourful pieces on the ground.

I dropped my sword and wiped the sweat from my forehead. With my hands resting on my knees, I looked up to see Luchia was wearing the biggest smile I'd ever seen.

'Have you seen this?' she asked, jumping up and down and pointing at her life monitor. 'We've completed Level 2! We've completed Level 2!'

'That's great news,' Archie said. 'What happens now?'

Before anyone said anything, a pair of yellow butterflies flew through the trees and settled on the ground beside us. I glanced around at the forest, trying to get one final look and then, moments later, we were home again.

I was so tired, I didn't even check the time on my watch. Instead, I sat on the carpet with my back resting against the green wall under the window.

'Did we really do all that?' I asked.

'Amazing, eh?' Archie replied.

'Yes,' I said. 'Thank you.'

'For what?'

'For getting us back in the game.'

After the day before at school, I probably should have been dreading going back. I was so happy though and I couldn't stop thinking about what we'd achieved.

66

'Good morning,' I said, startling Mrs Graham.

'Good morning, Matt,' she said, as she walked out of the classroom and closed the door behind her.

I made my way through the tightly packed tables and one of the girls smiled at me. She had long, wavy brown hair and friendly looking eyes. I hadn't spoken to her before but I knew who she was. I'd seen her in the classroom and in the playground and, just like me, she seemed to spend a lot of time on her own.

'Have you got a sister called Luchia?' she asked.

'Yes,' I said. 'How did you know that?'

'I met her at the library,' the girl replied. 'She said you were starting Witzengurgle at the same time as me.'

'That makes sense,' I said.

She tilted her head to one side. 'My name's Chloe by the way.'

'Hi, Chloe.'

'Where is she, Luchia I mean?' Chloe added. 'I thought Luchia was in the same class as us.'

'She's not very well,' I replied. 'Mum thinks it's scarlet fever.'

'Mum thinks it's scarlet fever,' said a sarcastic voice from the table in front of her. I looked up to see who it was, wondering for a moment whether it was Matt Parrot doing his repeating thing.

Unfortunately, it wasn't.

'Why do you have to be so rude all the time?' said Chloe. 'Scarlet fever is horrible.'

Calum looked at Chloe and then stared at me. 'I don't have to listen to her,' he said. 'I don't have to listen to anybody.'

On a normal day, I'm not sure what I'd have done in response. Today, however, was different. 'Good morning to you too, Calum,' I said, looking directly at him as I made my way back to my desk.

He obviously wasn't expecting me to be so friendly and he lowered his eyes. Then he looked up again and stared back with something that was far more intense than before. A cold wind crept its way into my clothes and I started to shiver.

'Is Anuska with him?' I said, as quietly as I could.

No response.

'Archie, are you there?'

Nothing, but then he whispered. 'Yes, I'm here.'

'Are you okay?'

'Fine,' he said, but he didn't sound fine. 'Anuska is wrapped around the table leg beneath Calum,' he said, his voice strained. 'Her fingers…are jabbing…into his ribs as though…she is trying to provoke…him.'

'What about you, Archie?' I asked. 'You sound terrible.'

'Yes…just…fighting her off,' he said.

I closed my eyes, immediately wishing I hadn't because Anuska's image appeared straight away. I could see her piercing green eyes above her veil and her slender grey figure swaying from side to side.

'Max, Max, Max,' said Calum, just as he'd done before in the playground. Again, he started quietly, but became louder and louder as the three Matts joined in.

'Max,' said a different, softer voice. I opened my eyes to see that Chloe had turned around.

'Ignore them, Max,' she said. 'They're just a bunch of weak and stupid boys.'

Chloe was right, but no matter how weak and stupid they were, they were winning. I could feel the smile beginning to slip from my face and I tried to force it back. Before long, it slipped away completely.

'Keep fighting,' Archie said, sounding a lot better. 'Think about the forest and our fight with the jesters. You can beat anything, Max.'

'I'll try,' I replied.

The chanting continued. 'Max, Max, Max,' and I placed my head into my hands.

'Why are they doing this?' I said.

'I don't know,' Archie said.

I suppose I already knew the answer even if I didn't want to admit it. As I've already found out, this is how bullies work. Once they think they've got you, they don't let go and try and push you lower than you ever thought possible.

The door slammed shut and thankfully the chanting stopped as Mrs Graham came back into the classroom. She wasn't on her own though. Beside her was a man wearing a blue jumper and holding an orange bicycle helmet.

'Settle down, Year 7s, settle down,' Mrs Graham said. 'We have a very special guest who has come to say a big thank you.'

He had black spiky hair that I recognised from somewhere. Then the memory of the accident flashed in my mind.

It was the man who'd been driving the black car that crashed into the wonky looking tree.

'Calum, would you like to come to the front please,' Mrs Graham said.

I glanced over at Calum, who was slowly lifting himself up.

'Calum, did you hear me? Please make your way to the front,' Mrs Graham continued.

He was confused I could tell and as he stood up, he glanced around the room. He looked at me for a moment and dropped back down into his seat. Immediately, the cold wind that had wrapped around me released itself.

'Calum, for the last time, will you stop hiding and come to the front of the class.'

'It's okay,' said the man in the blue jumper. 'I'll go and say hello.'

My real smile returned as the man stepped forward

and made his way through the classroom. He didn't even look at Calum but walked straight past his desk to where I was sitting.

'I want to thank you for saving my life,' he said. 'If there is anything, and I mean anything, I can do for you in the future, just let me know okay?'

Mrs Graham started waving. 'You've got the wrong boy, you've got the wrong boy,' she said.

'No I haven't,' he replied, without turning around. 'This is the young man all right. Is your name Calum?'

'No,' I said, standing up. 'It's Max.'

'Steve,' said the man, holding out a hand that I shook as firmly as I could.

CHAPTER 10

Steve left the classroom soon after and Mrs Graham carried on with the lesson. When the bell for break time sounded, I noticed that the spiky-haired man had returned and was standing at the front once again.

Calum jumped up from his desk and tried to duck his way out of the door.

'Not so fast,' Mrs Graham said to him. 'I'd like to have a word with you.'

She then turned her attention towards Steve. 'I'm so sorry for the misunderstanding.'

'No problem,' Steve said. 'Come on, Max, I need to show you something.'

As I walked out into the car park, I noticed Chloe

was beside me.

'Did Max really save your life?' she asked.

'I don't think I'd be here without him,' Steve replied. 'He was really brave too, much braver than I could have been.'

'Good for you, Max,' Chloe said, with a smile. 'Hopefully, Calum might leave you alone now.'

'Yes,' I replied, extremely pleased with myself all of a sudden, 'and thank you.'

Chloe headed off towards the main school building and, for a moment, I thought it would just be Steve and me. Then I heard the sound of someone singing as a few of the other boys followed us with Matt Hummingbird at the front.

'Is that your bike?' Matt Bellow asked, really loudly, as he pointed at the gleaming, white bicycle that leaned against the wall of the school hut. It had a slimline seat and bullhorn handle bars.

'Yes,' Steve replied. 'I bought it when I lost my car in the accident.'

'Is this what you wanted to show me?' I asked.

'Sort of,' said Steve, as he placed a finger against his mouth. 'Don't tell anyone, but I think this bike has special powers.'

'In what way?'

'One minute I was cycling to work,' he said. 'The next, there was a flash of blue and I was transported to Witzengurgle.'

'Can I have a go?' Matt Hummingbird asked.

'Can I have a go?' Matt Parrot repeated.

'Maybe one day,' Steve said. 'Max will have the first opportunity, if he wants.'

'That'd be great,' I replied, even though it did look a bit big for me.

'Ah, you're so lucky, Max,' Matt Bellow bellowed. 'I'd save someone's life if I could have a go on that.'

'See you soon, Max,' Steve said, as he put his helmet on. 'If you need anything in the meantime, you just let me know. Mrs Graham has all my contact details.'

He set off with one hand waving in the air. I don't really know what happened next. I may have stopped concentrating and it's possible I was seeing things. Either way, he'd barely gone ten metres, when there was this flash of blue and his bike seemed to disappear. I looked again, properly this time, and blinked. 'Did anyone else see that?' I asked.

'See what?' Matt Hummingbird replied.

I turned again and looked at the empty space where Steve and his bike had been.

'Are you sure none of you saw him disappear?' I asked.

They gathered together in a group and walked towards me. I stepped backwards, convinced they were about to start chanting my name again, but then noticed they were smiling.

'He seems all right,' said Matt Bellow, quietly for once, his long blonde fringe bobbing up and down as he spoke.

'Yea, he's pretty cool actually,' Matt Parrot said, for once not repeating the previous phrase.

The bell sounded to confirm that break time was over and we all headed back to the classroom. I slowed down a bit and let the others go in front.

'Archie,' I said. 'Have you any idea how Steve found

74

out where I go to school?'

'That would be telling, wouldn't it?' he said.

'I suppose the magic bike was your idea as well was it?'

'Maybe,' he said. 'I don't want to say too much.'

I smiled. 'Thank you.'

'You're welcome,' Archie replied.

Sometimes it really is amazing to have a guiding spirit!

'I'm sorry for the misunderstanding, Max,' said Mrs Graham, as I went into the classroom.

It was the first time she'd called me by the right name.

'Calum must have his reasons for what he did,' she continued. 'He's gone home now. Apparently, he's not feeling well.'

'Oh,' I said.

I couldn't believe my luck. He'd probably be back the next day, if not the day after, but at least I had a whole afternoon without him or Anuska to worry about.

'I think I'll leave you for a while,' said Archie, as I walked to my desk. 'All that stuff with the magic bike has tired me out.'

'Okay,' I said, as quietly as I could. 'That's fine.'

Without Calum, the next lesson seemed to fly by. Mrs Graham was particularly pleasant. She kept on coming over to my desk and apologising for the misunderstanding with Steve and the accident.

'It's all right,' I told her, more times than I remember.

Anyway, it all meant that when the bell sounded, I

was actually looking forward to lunchtime for the first time since I'd started at Witzengurgle.

'Do you mind if I sit with you?' asked Chloe, as I headed to the canteen.

Once we started chatting we couldn't stop. It helped that we had things in common. For one, we were new to the school and secondly, we both like to put cheese and onion crisps into our sandwiches.

'Do you watch much TV?' she asked.

'Sometimes,' I replied. 'But not that much.'

'What else do you do?'

I did think about it for a while. I was about to tell her about my building blocks, but I decided that it might sound a bit boring.

'I play a game,' I said. 'It's not just any game though.'

I know I probably shouldn't have, but we were getting on so well; I told her everything: about the seaspirits, the vampire berserkers and even the knight. I didn't think she'd believe me but she asked loads of questions.

'It sounds great,' she said.

'Yes,' I replied, 'it really is.'

'How was your day, Max?' Mum asked, as I walked through the door a few hours later.

'Eventful,' I replied. As always, I could have said an awful lot more. As always, however, she looked so tired and the last thing I wanted to do was burden her with my stuff.

After tea, Mum went to watch TV in the living

room and I carefully and quietly made my way up the stairs and into Luchia's room.

'Are you awake?' I asked.

'No,' she replied.

'Very funny,' I said, as I sat on the floor. 'I was thinking about Level 3 today. Surely it won't be long before we can have a go.'

'I hope not,' she replied.

I could sense Archie was there too. 'I don't suppose you've spoken to the knight, have you?' I asked.

'Not yet,' he said. 'Maybe we could all go and speak to him together.'

I stood up. 'Sounds like a good plan to me.'

I gently closed Luchia's door and tiptoed across the landing. After heading downstairs, I pulled my box of building blocks to the middle of the room and started to add a few pieces to the castle. Although I'd finished most of the wall and the turrets, I'd barely even thought about the inside, particularly in the castle towers. So, I added a spiral staircase and a couple of rooms.

Unfortunately, I didn't get the chance to finish them.

'Here we go,' Archie said, as the room started to spin and turn to darkness. When I opened my eyes, I was standing on the drawbridge that led to the portcullis.

The knight was there, sitting on Galahad, whose tail flashed in the evening sunlight.

'Can I help you, peasant?' he asked, with a rather disdainful look on his face.

'I hope so,' I said. 'When can we start Level 3?'

'Oh that,' he said. 'You're too late.'

'Too late for what?' Luchia asked.

'It's an odd thing,' the knight said. 'A different peasant by the name of Calum and his grey witch Anuska told me you wanted them to play the level.'

'Play the level?' I asked, wondering for a moment whether I'd caught the copying disease from Matt Parrot.

'I don't understand,' Luchia said. 'Who are these people?'

'Calum goes to school with Max,' said Archie. 'Anuska is a friend of Calum's.'

I looked at Archie and back at the knight.

'It still doesn't make sense,' I said. 'Why would we want them to play the level for us?'

'I wondered that too,' said the knight. 'But they had a girl with them, Chloe I think she was called. She seemed to have great knowledge about everything.'

My heart sank.

'Chloe,' said Luchia. 'The girl I met in the library?'

'Maybe,' the knight said. 'She said she knew you. She also mentioned she knew Max from school and that playing the game on your behalf would be the honourable thing to do.'

Luchia and Archie looked directly at me.

'I thought she was a friend,' I said. 'We were talking at lunchtime today and I told her about the game a bit.'

'Max,' Luchia said. 'This was supposed to be our secret.'

I turned to the knight. 'I didn't think she even liked Calum. Anyway, he went home before I'd even spoken to Chloe.'

78

'Don't ask me,' the knight replied. 'He did mention something about a clever tactic he'd managed to contrive, but that's all I know I'm afraid.'

I couldn't believe it.

'Surely our game isn't over completely,' Luchia said. 'Surely, we get another go, don't we?'

The knight grabbed at the reins of his horse. 'All you can do is wait, and hope they fail in their quest.'

'It doesn't seem right,' said Archie. 'Okay, maybe Max shouldn't have told Chloe about the game but it's not as though we've done anything wrong.'

The knight kicked his stirrup into the belly of his white horse and turned towards me. 'I'm afraid this is not strictly true,' he said. 'Are you going to tell them, Max, or shall I?'

I knew straight away what he meant. 'I showed Chloe the life monitor.'

'Oh no, Max,' said Luchia. 'Please tell me you didn't.'

'She seemed so interested,' I replied, my mood sinking further into embarrassment. 'I thought I'd show it to her to prove I was telling the truth.'

'And do you remember what I said would happen if you did such a thing?' the knight asked, his tone of voice as cold and angry as I'd ever heard.

'Something about severe consequences,' Archie said.

'Exactly,' said the knight, 'and because Max has broken one of the fundamental rules I so clearly laid down at the beginning, others have been allowed to take your place in the game.'

'You certainly have made things a lot more interesting,' the knight said, the anger in his voice beginning to subside. 'Anyway, much as I'd like to stay here and chat, I need to find some arms for a coat I'm making.'

'You will remember where we are though, won't you?' Archie said.

'I'll think about it,' the knight said, before turning towards me. 'In the meantime, try not to show your life monitor to anyone else. The last thing I need is another load of peasants turning up, asking me if they can have a go.'

Galahad reared, the front hooves circling and

clicking together, before the white horse galloped through the portcullis and up the stone steps towards the castle.

'I guess we'd better go and work something out between us,' Archie said.

Luchia, however, was more direct. 'You should have spoken to me before you started telling people about our game.'

'I'm sorry.'

'You must realise how much this means to me,' Luchia continued, 'it's all I have at the moment.'

I felt terrible. Not only for Luchia, but for Archie too. I'd blamed him for so many things in the past and yet this time it was definitely my fault. As I looked up, a pair of yellow butterflies fluttered past and the castle, the forest and everything else faded into memories.

'It'll be all right, Max, you'll see,' Archie said, as we arrived back home.

'How can you be so sure?' I asked, picking up a few of the building blocks and throwing them into the box as hard as I could.

I left the back room and walked past the living room where flickers of light from the TV screen flashed into the corridor. With careful steps, I headed up the stairs, took a deep breath and nudged into Luchia's room.

'Are you awake?' I asked, as I peered into the darkness.

'No,' Luchia replied.

'I'm really sorry,' I said, uncertain whether I'd be invited in.

'Calum seems like a nightmare,' she said, and

81

turned on her bedside lamp. 'I can't believe he'd make such an effort to play Ma-Chia.'

I knelt on the floor beside her bed. 'For some reason, ever since I beat him in a scavenger hunt, he's been really angry at me.'

'Oh,' said Luchia. "That's a bit mean.'

'Also, Anuska hates Archie,' I said.

Luchia sat up. 'In which case, we should definitely make sure we beat them.'

'But how?'

'I've been thinking,' said Luchia. 'You know how annoyed the knight was about the life monitor?'

'Yes,' I replied. 'Sorry about that.'

'It doesn't matter,' she said. 'Anyway, you know the knight told us we'd made things a bit more interesting.'

'Yea, so what?'

Luchia smiled. 'When we first wrote the game, we added some interesting extras, do you remember? Well I think we might be able to sneak back in.'

'I don't like the sound of this,' Archie said.

'It might be a risk,' said Luchia. 'But I think the knight is testing us.'

'And he seems keen for us to do well,' I said. 'He's even said he likes us.'

'Exactly,' said Luchia.

'You're forgetting one important thing,' said Archie. 'At the moment, we are locked out of the game.'

'Maybe not for long,' said Luchia.

'Even locked things can be unlocked sometimes,' I said, beginning to believe that Luchia may be right.

She rolled out of bed onto the floor and lifted the purple-coloured rulebook I'd previously shown to

Archie from her bedside cabinet.

'Do you think this might help?' she asked.

Using my blue dyslexic ruler she'd been keeping as a bookmark, I read the paragraph she was pointing at. 'It's a bit extreme.'

'If it's our only way in, it might be worth it,' Luchia replied.

'What is?' Archie said.

Luchia looked at me again. 'If we wait, the others will have completed Level 3, then 4.'

'What happens if we make any mistakes?' I said, as I read the paragraph for a second time.

'Then we never come home and we stay in the game forever,' Luchia said, confirming what I already knew.

'Hold on,' Archie said, 'did you say forever?'

I could tell he was about to go into serious mode. 'I know you're supposed to be our guiding spirit,' I said.

'That's right,' Archie replied. 'It is therefore my job to offer advice. You may not always choose to accept it, but the advice is there nonetheless.'

'The thing is, you're not just our guiding spirit anymore, you're also our friend.'

'That's a very kind thing to say,' Archie said. 'Even so, being stuck in the game doesn't seem right to me.'

'Like I said before,' Luchia said. 'It's a risk and if we do this, we'll need your help in so many ways.'

'She's right, Archie.'

'Please, Archie, please,' Luchia said. 'Sometimes, everybody has to take a chance, don't they?'

The longer the silence continued, the more convinced I became that he was about to refuse.

'You're not the only ones who could get into serious trouble with this,' he said, in a stern and sincere manner.

'But?' Luchia asked.

'But,' he said, his tone much brighter this time. 'As it's you two, why not!'

Luchia wrote down a series of numbers and letters on a piece of paper.

'The password,' she said.

'Can anyone explain how this is supposed to work?' Archie asked.

'Most games have a debug menu,' I said. 'It means the designer can test the game and make sure it's working properly in the development stage.'

'No, that hasn't helped,' Archie replied. 'Someone is going to have to explain this a bit slower I'm afraid.'

'New games have more faults than most, in fact, every game we've ever played has had a fault or two,' Luchia said. 'When we wrote the script for this, I added a debugging function to make it seem a bit more real.'

'And then you came along and the game became a reality,' I said.

'Oh, that's great,' Archie replied, 'I still don't understand what's going on and yet somehow, it's all my fault.'

Nothing happened at first and the three of us just sat there, staring at the piece of paper.

'I don't think it's working,' I said.

'Maybe the locked thing can't be unlocked after all,' Archie said.

Luchia rolled her eyes. 'Try and be patient.'

I didn't feel like being patient. It didn't help that Archie kept saying such ridiculous things. Then the piece of paper started to shimmer and the light faded to darkness.

'Forget what I said a few moments ago,' said Archie, as the room began to spin. 'Get ready for lift off!'

As always, I closed my eyes. For the first time, I also crossed my fingers. When I opened my eyes, we were no longer in our comfortable world of carpets and wallpaper. Instead, we were back in amongst the trees that were so tightly packed together I could barely move. I pushed forward and squeezed past a drooping branch that was thick with pine needles.

'This place has changed a bit,' Luchia said.

It wasn't only the trees. The pathway had disappeared and we were surrounded by brambles that scratched at my legs as I walked. Ferns sprouted their jagged green leaves in every direction.

'Does anyone have any idea where to go?' Archie asked. 'Assuming anyone can see anything.'

'We should head for the mountain,' Luchia said, 'which I think is this way.'

I followed her through the dense forest, my shoulders and arms brushing against the lower branches as I went. Eventually, I caught her up.

'Are you sure this is right?' I asked, as we crossed a wooden bridge over a stream.

'Not really,' she replied. 'I was a bit worried Archie might take us back if we didn't keep moving.'

'Has the game done all this,' I asked, 'because of the debugging?'

'I think so.'

I pushed past another heavy branch and kicked my way through the ferns.

'Ouch,' said a voice,

'Who said that?' I asked.

'Said what?' Luchia snapped.

'It doesn't matter.'

I looked down to see movement beneath my feet. Then I noticed that the fern I'd just kicked was squeezing its way out of the ground. After lifting its leaves, it used its roots like feet to scamper away from me.

Certain I was seeing things, I shook my head. As I continued walking, I noticed some of the brown pinecones in the trees had small black circles like eyes. They were standing on the branches and appeared to be pointing in our direction.

A flash of movement caused me to look down to see a strand of ivy rushing across the ground. Before I could move, its tendrils wrapped themselves around my ankles.

'Get off!' I shouted.

With a sharp tug, my feet were pulled from underneath me and I bumped onto the ground. The ivy tightened its grip and, with a jerk, it dragged me along the forest floor. Slowly at first, then gathering speed until finally, with my face bruised and my mouth filled with earth, I came to a stop.

I looked up to see Archie and Luchia fighting their way through the trees.

'Okay, you get one side and I'll get the other,' Luchia said.

In response, the ivy dragged me along for a second time. Once again, Luchia and Archie raced after me and this time, when they caught up, they ripped it from my ankles. In response, the ivy cried a loud yelp of pain and rushed away into the undergrowth.

'Just in time,' said Archie.

'For what?' I asked, but then I saw it. A deep black hole the ivy had been dragging me towards. I stood up, picked up a stone and threw it into the abyss. I threw in another one, expecting to hear the clatter as it struck the bottom. It was a sound that never came.

'Come on, we need to go!' shouted Luchia. 'Otherwise they'll catch us up.'

'They?' said Archie.

'The multi-coloured people with the big smiling mouths,' Luchia added, pointing at a pair of jesters who were bursting through the trees.

'Take one of these,' Archie said, handing me a sword. 'I kept them from the last level.'

'Why didn't you use them on the ivy?' Luchia asked.

'It just didn't seem right somehow,' Archie replied, as he handed one to Luchia too.

Swords flashing, we cut a path through the forest. Every now and then, I heard a shout of 'Excuse me!' and 'Do you mind what you're doing with that thing!'

I didn't reply but kept going until I was simply too tired to go any further.

'I think we've lost them,' said Archie, as he stopped beside me.

I slumped onto the ground. 'That's lucky, because

I'm shattered.'

'Sssshhh,' said Luchia,' or they might hear us.'

I knelt, rested my head against the cold bark of a tree and shut my eyes. I was so tired I could have fallen asleep where I was.

'Over here!' a voice shouted.

'Yoo hoo! This way,' said a different voice.

'Be quiet, Max,' said Luchia. 'The jesters will find us.'

'It's not me,' I protested.

'I've found them,' another voice, this time coming from the branches in the tree I was resting against.

'It's the forest,' Archie confirmed.

'This is crazy,' Luchia said. 'Come on, we'd better keep going.'

'They're getting away!' came another shout from the forest.

My lungs burning, my head spinning, I forced myself into a run. Barely able to lift my feet, I tripped on a protruding root, slipped and crashed into a heap. I was about to push myself up when I heard a second crash and a third one. When I looked around, both Luchia and Archie were lying beside me.

CHAPTER 13

A female jester bounded towards us. In response, Luchia pushed herself up from the ground and swiped her sword. With a jangle of bells, the jester shattered into a pile of colourful pieces.

'Come on, Max,' said Archie.

'There's too many of them,' I said.

'Don't give up,' Luchia pleaded, as one of the jesters continued to bound and jump in a really annoying way.

'I don't want to fight it anymore,' I said.

'What are you talking about?' Archie asked.

'I've had enough,' I said, 'and anyway, I've got a better idea.'

I stood up and hacked my way through the trees and the thorny stems of bramble. The others followed and together we created a narrow corridor that led us to the place where the ivy had grabbed hold of my ankles.

'What's going on, Max?' Luchia asked.

'Whatever it is, it has to work,' said Archie.

'I know,' I replied. 'You two need to stand on the other side of the pit and I'll stand here.'

'Then what?' Luchia asked.

'Then we wait.'

'Are you sure about this?' Archie asked.

'No, but I have to try.'

I could tell neither Archie nor Luchia had complete faith in me. Even so, they did as I asked. Luckily, one of the trees did exactly as I hoped.

'This way,' it said.

'They're trapped,' said another. 'Come on!'

'Thanks for the reminder,' I said, but the second tree was right. I looked along the narrow corridor we'd created and laid my sword on the ground.

The first jester bounded towards me. He leapt through the air and I ducked, just in time to allow him to fall into the pit behind me. I heard him scream, but the noise faded as he descended further into the abyss.

I stood up, ducked again as another one followed, this time accompanied by the jingle of bells and she too disappeared. Another one followed, then another, as though they were unable to stop themselves from obeying their natural instinct to attack. Occasionally, one would appear from behind Archie and Luchia and they too dived to the ground as the jesters vanished

92

into the pit of nothingness.

'Keep going, Max,' I heard Luchia shout, as the flow of colourful jesters reduced to twos and ones until, finally, they stopped coming.

'Is that all of them?' Luchia asked.

'I don't know,' I replied, and flinched as a figure pushed its way through the trees. I was just about to get back into position, when I noticed the glint of light on the shiny breastplate.

The knight wandered over. 'Not bad for a peasant,' he said, shaking my hand.

'Max, you've done it,' said Archie. 'You've beaten them.'

'I just needed to stop fighting that's all.'

'I have to say, Max,' said Luchia, 'that was really clever.'

'Thanks,' I said, 'it's not often I get told I'm clever.'

'Not as clever as I am,' the knight said. He was holding the sword I'd dropped on the ground in the forest. 'The one who retrieves Excalibur from the clan of colourful people shall be known, forevermore, as Sir Percival.'

'Isn't that your sword, Max?'

'Ssshhh,' I said.

I've always believed that sometimes, allowing people to have their moment is simply the best thing to do.

'Right, anyway, as glorious a melee as that all was, we need to move on to more important matters,' Sir Percival said. 'It's time I gave you these.'

'What are they?' asked Archie.

'New life monitors,' he said, handing them to each

of us. 'They're a bit more sensitive than the others.'

'How do you mean?' I asked.

'The life-source will drain far more rapidly, which means they'll go into red much sooner.'

'How can that be fair?' Archie asked.

'Fair? Who said anything about being fair?' Sir Percival continued. 'Interesting idea of yours to use a debug menu. However, as you may have already noticed, the game has been modified as a result.'

'There's a clock on mine,' Luchia said, looking at her screen. 'A kind of egg timer.'

'Oh that,' said the knight. 'Yes, from now on, you will also be fighting against time.'

'And if we run out of time?' Archie said.

'Then your quest will be over,' Sir Percival said, 'and you will never go home.'

'Just like that?' asked Archie.

'Just like that,' the knight replied.

'But how will we know when we've finished a level?' I asked. 'Will you set us a target?'

Sir Percival scrunched the palms of his chainmailed gloves together. 'You will know when you've finished a level,' he said. 'Because I will tell you.'

'Thanks,' said Luchia.

'I have, however, decided to give you a small opportunity for success,' the knight continued. 'Your life monitors can now be used to reduce things.'

'Things?' I asked.

'Items you may want to keep,' the knight replied. 'Press the blue button on the monitor and hey presto, the items will reduce in size. Press it again and the item expands once more.'

94

'Like a table you mean?' I asked.

Sir Percival tilted his head. 'If you did happen to locate a round table, that would indeed be most welcome.'

'Is there anything else you can tell us?' Archie asked. 'Apart from the new rules and the stuff about the reducer thing.'

'The others aren't far in front of you,' the knight replied, 'and you have a friend within their group who is slowing them down.'

'Who?' I asked.

'You should know,' he replied.

'Chloe?' I said. 'It's Chloe, isn't it?'

'But why?' Luchia asked.

Sir Percival started to walk away. 'This is for you to ascertain,' he said. 'The good news is that from now on, there won't be any more jesters for you to concern yourselves about.'

'That should make things easier,' said Archie.

'Maybe,' said the knight, in a strange tone. 'Anyway, you have different enemies now, one of which is time. Tick tock, tick tock.'

CHAPTER 14

'New enemies,' I said. 'I wonder what or who they'll be.'

'Try not to think about it,' said Archie. 'Who knows what that imagination of yours might create.'

'Well, whatever it is, it'll be dark soon so we need to find some supplies,' said Luchia, 'and don't forget to keep checking your monitors.'

I didn't even look at my screen and started to search through the ferns, the brambles and under the branches.

'You won't find any ration packs here,' said one of the ferns.

'Thanks,' I said, but then we crossed the wooden

bridge over the stream and headed away from the talking forest.

As the sun lowered and hid itself behind the trees, I felt a shiver. With a feeling of dread, I closed my eyes. Luckily there was no sign of the green-eyed Anuska.

'Are you okay, Max?' Archie asked, walking beside me.

'I think so,' I said, as another chill wind crept under my clothes. 'Do you mind if I ask you something?'

'No,' he replied. 'Go ahead.'

'Who exactly is Anuska?'

Archie stopped, looked up and then carried on walking. 'She is Calum's guiding spirit,' he replied, 'someone your imagination managed to release.'

'Yes, I know that bit, but who is she, really?'

He didn't say anything for a while but stared straight ahead as we pushed our way through the pine trees.

'In human terms, let's just say we both went to the same school,' he said. 'Given the opportunity to choose our next class, she did one subject and I did another.'

'A good and bad thing then?'

'It's a bit more complicated than that,' Archie replied, pausing for a moment. 'You see, it wasn't actually her choice to do the other subject.'

'Whose was it then?'

'I kind of tricked her, then pretended I'd made a mistake,' Archie replied. 'At the time, it got me into a huge amount of trouble. Then you and Luchia came along to give me the chance to put things right.'

'But how?'

'I believe the human word is redemption.'

Archie took a step away to confirm our conversation was over. I didn't know what to think. If I understood him correctly, he'd just admitted it was his fault that Anuska was the way she was. It didn't seem real somehow and I looked over at him, trying to think of the right thing to say. There was something about him though, something a bit closed. It was as though he was making a special effort to be left alone.

As I looked a bit closer I noticed something else. When I'd first met him, he seemed a bit hunched up with his head bowed. Now, however, his back was straight, his body upright. It was as though, by telling me the truth, a huge weight had been lifted from his shoulders.

I carried on looking for ration packs and almost immediately I found one with some food in. The others found some too and after a while we came to a small gap in the trees that was big enough for us all to sit down.

'Look what I've found,' Luchia said, waving a silver saucepan. 'Have we got enough for a soup yet?'

'Maybe,' I said. 'I've found some mushrooms, peppers and cabbage.'

'Tomatoes too,' said Archie.

We emptied the contents of our ration packs into the silver pan.

'I've found some matches,' said Archie, looking much happier. He gathered a few sticks and twigs into the shape of a fire.

There are probably several reasons why we'd made such a big mistake. It might have been because we were talking. It might have been because it was getting dark, but even so, there's no real excuse. There's a big difference between a ration pack with apples on it and one with a picture of skull and crossbones. Even so, one of us had missed it.

'Put it out,' shouted Luchia.

I stamped on the fire, but it was already too late. A huge cloud of luminous red smoke formed itself into a spiral that was heading towards the branches at the top of the trees.

'We need to get going,' Luchia said.
'But we haven't eaten,' I replied.

'Luchia's right,' Archie said. 'That smoke could attract almost anything.'

We set off into the deepening gloom, cutting our way through the trees until, at last, the trunks and branches started to separate. The light from a full moon led us to a clearing of long grass about the same size as a football pitch.

Thump…Thump.

'What's that?' I said.

'Something big,' said Archie. 'Any ideas, Max?'

Thump…Thump.

We dived onto the ground.

'No,' I said.

As the noise became louder, we crept on our hands and knees through the long, green stems. I looked over to see that Luchia was beside me. As I looked the other way, I realised we were on our own.

'Have you seen Archie?' I asked, stopping for a moment.

'No, but he can't be that far away, surely.'

Using our elbows, we dragged ourselves through the field until we came to the edge of the grass. I was about to stand up and run to the forest, when I noticed a figure in the shadows of the trees. As I looked again, I realised it was Chloe. She was about ten metres away with a rope tied around her waist.

'It's a trap,' I said, as Anuska slithered behind the tree to which Chloe was tied.

Luchia looked at me and back towards Chloe.

'I think you're right,' she said, 'but we've got to do something. We can't just leave her there.'

'We should split up,' I said, but then I saw Archie.

He was about twenty metres away from where we were lying. He was at a different angle from us and so it's possible he didn't have a great view of where Anuska was slithering.

'Is that Calum?' Luchia asked.

I looked towards the trees.

'Yes,' I replied. He was standing beside Anuska and smiling one of his annoying smiles of self-congratulation.

'Have you got anything left?' Luchia asked.

I checked inside my rucksack and my pockets too. The only thing I found was my life monitor.

'Oh no,' I said. 'I'm down to my last bar of green.'

Luchia checked her rucksack as well. 'I suppose we'll have to try this and see what happens,' she said, holding a stick of dynamite in her hand.

'No way,' I said.

'Have you got any other ideas?' Luchia asked.

She'd barely finished speaking when Archie stood up and started running towards the trees.

'Cross your fingers!' Luchia said, as she lit the end of the wick.

I looked over to see that Archie had not only reached Chloe, he'd also untied the bandage from around her mouth.

'Leave me alone,' Chloe shouted, but before Archie could reply, Anuska had slithered towards him.

I didn't see anything more, for a few seconds at least. Luchia threw the dynamite into the air and I ducked down, held my hands over my ears and waited for the BOOM!

CHAPTER 15

Once the ground had stopped trembling and the dust from the explosion had dispersed into the moonlit sky, I pushed myself up.

'Come on!' said Luchia, her shadow racing along beside her.

After reaching the trees, I searched left, then right but Calum and Anuska were nowhere to be seen. Archie was leaning against a rock and although he looked a bit dazed, he didn't appear to be injured.

'Was that one of our new enemies?' he asked, as I went towards him.

'No,' I said. 'It was dynamite.'

Luchia, meanwhile, was kneeling beside Chloe.

'She's fainted,' Luchia said.

Archie came over and sat beside them both. He placed his ear next to Chloe's mouth and checked her pulse.

'She'll be all right,' he said, placing her limp body high on his back and over his shoulders, piggyback style.

As he did so, a gust of wind swept past us into the forest. It dislodged a branch that creaked and fell to the ground with a loud crack. We crouched as low as we could.

'Is that them?' Luchia said. 'Calum and Anuska I mean.'

'It's possible,' said Archie. 'They could be anywhere and we need to get going.'

Under the light of the moon and a thousand stars, we set off along a muddy track at the edge of the forest. I felt a shiver and slowed down to let the others go in front. I closed my eyes. Luckily, there was no sign of the grey woman with the green eyes.

'I think it's okay to go into the trees now,' I said.

'What makes you say that?' Luchia asked.

'Just a feeling,' I replied.

With careful steps and our heads bowed, we headed into the gloom of overhanging, finger-like branches in the forest. We hadn't gone far when Archie stopped.

'I need a moment,' he said. 'For an eleven-year-old, this young lady doesn't half weigh a lot.'

As we stood there, I thought about something important. In the moments before the explosion, I remembered how my life monitor had hovered at one bar of green. I lifted it from my pocket.

'I've got four bars,' I said, thinking aloud. 'How's everyone else doing?'

Luchia rubbed her fingers across her monitor.

'I've got four bars as well,' she said, 'and according to my timer, we've still got about two hours to finish the level.'

'Something strange is going on,' I said.

'Isn't there always?' Archie replied. 'Come on, let's keep going.'

We quickened our step, even though each foot we placed in front of the other was harder work than the last as by now we'd started to climb. Soon after, we left the forest and headed along a wider path. On one side was the upward slope of a mountain. On the other was a steep drop to the valley below.

'Wow, look at that!' Luchia said.

I looked up to see a crown of jagged rock on top of the mountains in the distance. The moon appeared to be sitting on the crown as though it was having a rest.

'It's so peaceful,' Archie said. 'I could stand here forever.'

'BOO!' shouted a voice behind us.

I think Archie's scream was the loudest. Mine was probably second and Luchia's third.

Once I'd jumped back into my skin, I turned to see a shiny breastplate and the smiling face of the knight.

'You really scared me,' I said.

'My apologies, peasant,' Sir Percival replied. 'I couldn't resist it.'

'Thanks,' said Archie.

'I have some information,' the knight continued,

'useful information in fact, because you have succeeded in your quest to complete Level 3.'

I smiled. Archie laid Chloe on the ground and Luchia started giggling in the way she does when she's really excited.

'What about Calum and Anuska?' I asked.

'Ah the black knight and the witch,' Sir Percival replied. 'For now, their adventure is at an end.'

'Shame,' said Archie. 'But why?'

'They chose to play the game in a dishonourable manner,' the knight said. 'I have warned you about this haven't I?'

'How do we know when we're playing it in the right way?' I asked.

Sir Percival didn't reply but kicked at the stone path with his metal boots. 'Questions, questions. All of a sudden you are a barrelful of questions. Right, my turn. Have you checked Chloe's life monitor?'

Archie lifted the device from her pocket. He looked at the screen and handed it over to me.

'It's still green. All five bars are still green,' I said.

'It's because she tried to help us isn't it?' said Luchia.

'Oh I get it,' said Archie, 'and then, because we rescued her, we've had our life restored.'

'Hooray! It's about time you understood the true nature of your pursuit for glory,' said the knight. 'Sorry, I meant to say that this is most intuitive of you.'

'Thank you,' said Luchia.

'There's some more good news too,' Sir Percival continued. 'Because we haven't had time to set up Level 4 yet, you all get the chance to go home.'

'For how long?' I asked.

'I don't know, I haven't decided. We could call you at any time,' the knight replied. 'It's going to be difficult though, far more arduous than anything you've experienced so far.'

'One more question,' said Archie. 'The noise we heard in the forest, the Thump, Thump. What was it?'

Sir Percival took off his helmet, his long blonde hair resting on his shoulders. 'The mountain giant you mean.'

'Giant?' I said.

'That's right,' said the knight, 'but you don't have to worry about him. Not for a while anyway.'

'But he seemed so close,' Luchia said.

'He was tempted by your ridiculous bonfire,' Sir Percival replied. 'Even so, I would have been surprised if he'd found you. Man-eating, fifty-metre-high giants don't tend to leave the mountains very often.'

'Man-eating,' I said, followed by a gasp.

'Fifty-metre-high,' said Luchia, her eyes wide open.

'Giant,' Archie said, his blue colour fading to white.

'Yes,' said the knight. 'Terrifying isn't he?'

No one had the chance to reply as the next time I looked up, a pair of yellow butterflies fluttered past. I closed my eyes and when I opened them, we'd been transported back to Luchia's room once again.

'What do you think we should do now?' Archie asked.

'Max should get out of here or else Mum will be angry,' Luchia said, 'and don't forget to plug in your life monitors.'

106

Monday arrived and all I wanted to do was speak to Chloe and make sure she hadn't been hurt in the explosion. Unfortunately, when her name was called out on the register, she was marked as absent.

So I stayed behind at break time.

'She has a headache and is not feeling very well,' Mrs Graham told me. 'It sounds a bit like flu.'

It all seemed a bit convenient to me. The more I thought about it, the more I was convinced her illness had something to do with the game.

'Max, are you with us?' Mrs Graham said a few times during English and I nodded, even though I wasn't. I suppose I could have tried to explain things to her but, like most adults, there's no way she'd have understood. At least she was still calling me by the right name.

Calum was unusually quiet. I tried to say hello a couple of times but he didn't reply. In fact, ever since Steve had been into school, he'd hardly spoken to anyone and that included his so-called friends. One of them, Matt Bellow, had even moved away from Calum to the desk in front of me.

'Does that blue ruler thing help you to read?' he asked, a bit too loudly for my liking.

'Something like that,' I replied and looked in the opposite direction.

'Sorry,' he said, slightly quieter this time. 'I didn't mean to be annoying or anything.'

I've always been sensitive about my dyslexia. There are worse things in life I know but when someone mentions it, I can't help getting defensive. Then I thought about the battle with the jesters in the forest. I remembered how I'd decided not to fight and instead made them jump into the abyss of a bottomless pit.

All of a sudden, everything seemed okay again.

'Yes,' I said. 'It stops the words from jumping around the page.'

It was probably the first time I'd spoken about dyslexia without getting angry. Anyway, it wasn't Matt's fault I'd found school so difficult—that was down to Calum. Archie, on the other hand, blamed everything on Calum's guiding spirit.

'Is Anuska here, Archie?' I asked, once Matt had turned around. 'I can't sense her anymore.'

'Yes,' he replied. 'She's hiding below Calum's table. She seems hurt somehow, as though she's suffering from an injury.'

'Probably her ego,' I said.

It was Friday when Chloe turned up at school. She didn't look well and had dark rims around her eyes, just like Luchia's.

'Thanks for everything,' Calum grunted, under his breath, as she walked past his desk. Chloe ignored him. As the lesson continued, I kept looking in her direction but no matter how much I tried, she ignored me as well.

'Now's your chance,' said Archie when the break time bell sounded and I followed Chloe out of the classroom.

As I walked behind her, she quickened her step and rushed into the girls' changing room in the sports hall. I waited outside on one of benches for what seemed like ages.

'Are you okay?' I asked, when she came out.

Chloe glanced at me, her eyes alert and full of panic. For a moment, I thought she was going to make a run for it.

'Mrs Graham told me you had the flu,' I said.

She didn't say anything at first, but without looking at me, she started to speak. 'I didn't know Calum would do what he did. He told me you were playing some game and asked me to find out a bit more about it.'

'Typical Calum,' I said.

'I've been struggling to make friends this year,' she said, 'and so when he asked me to meet him after school, I thought he was being nice.'

'I don't think that's possible. For Calum to be nice I mean.'

'I know that now and, in fact, I think he'll do anything to get his own way. I'm sorry I told him so much. I didn't realise it was all going to be so real.'

'Don't worry,' I said. 'If someone had told me about the game, I wouldn't have believed them either.'

Her face was bright red, her water-filled eyes flicking in all directions.

'Everything started to spin, we were all in the forest and all these people in coloured suits started jumping around,' she said. 'Then the hideous snake thing that follows Calum started telling me to do things. It was horrible.'

She sat down beside me on the bench.

'Thank you for trying to help us,' I said.

'I can only remember little bits, but when I said I

couldn't help them anymore, the snake woman wrapped herself around me and put me into some sort of trance. The next thing I knew, I was attached to the tree and a blue man was running towards me. Then there was this loud boom.'

'The man is a friend of mine called Archie. The boom was dynamite,' I said.

'Please say sorry to Luchia, ' Chloe said. 'Without her help, I don't know what I would have done.'

'Oh, what did she do?'

'We were in the library,' said Chloe, looking far more relaxed, 'our mums were talking adult stuff, so Luchia and me went shopping. Then this siren went off and people started running, screaming and shouting.'

'She didn't tell me this.'

'It was only a fire alarm but I must have fainted, like I did in the forest. When I woke up, your sister was telling me to stay calm and take deep breaths.'

'She does that sort of thing when Mum has one of her panic attacks,' I said. 'I think the doctor told her how to do it.'

'It doesn't surprise me,' Chloe replied. 'She was brilliant.'

'Just a thought,' said Archie, interrupting. 'If Anuska can get Chloe into the game, so can I. Why don't you ask her if she wants to join us on the next level?'

I couldn't reply to Archie of course. Not right then anyway, because Chloe would have wondered who I was talking to. So, without thinking, I did as he asked. 'You can carry on with the game if you like,' I said, 'on our side this time.'

Her face lit up. 'Really?' she said. 'You'd let me do that?'

'You need to be sure though. It won't be easy.'

'Wow! Thank you,' Chloe replied.

The bell sounded to signal the end of break. We headed out of the sports hall and back towards the wooden hut.

'Why did you want me to ask her to join us?' I whispered to Archie once I'd sat down in the classroom. 'It could be dangerous.'

'I think we're going to need all the help we can get,' he replied.

'But what if things go wrong?'

'Well, hopefully they won't.'

'Oh great,' I said. 'That's really comforting.'

When I got home I did my double-back thing on the landing and headed into Luchia's room to give her an update.

'Archie's asked Chloe to join us,' I said.

'Good,' Luchia said.

'Archie seemed pleased as well,' I replied.

Luchia didn't say anything else and rolled over away from me.

'Are you all right?' I said.

'It's worse today,' she said. 'I'm beginning to think I may never get any better.'

'Don't say that,' I said, but if I'm honest, she didn't look well at all.

As I came out of Luchia's room, Mum was on the landing waiting for me. At first, I thought I was in trouble but I noticed the look on her face wasn't one of anger but something else. It was a happy look I hadn't seen for a long time.

'I had a visitor today,' she said.

'Who?'

'A man called Steve. Apparently, I should be proud of you, but as I didn't know what he was talking about, I couldn't really say anything.'

'Oh, sorry,' I said. 'I must have forgotten.'

'Forgotten?' she said, with an obvious tone of frustration. 'You save someone's life and then you forget to tell your mum. How does that happen?'

'You seem so busy these days,' I said, almost without thinking. 'I honestly didn't think you'd be interested.'

Mum leant against the wall and brushed her hand through her hair. 'I could say that's not fair, Max; I could get really angry with you for what you've just said but I won't.'

'Sorry,' I replied. 'But it's how I feel.'

I could have also mentioned that there were far more important things going on. I could have told her about Level 4 and that there will be giants, vampire berserkers and seaspirits chasing us around. I could have said that if we get it wrong, we may never come home, but I decided not to...I know how things like that can affect her sometimes.

'He gave me this,' Mum said, handing me a business card, 'and when he'd gone, I spoke to the school to check the details with them.'

She paused for a moment and her expression changed. 'Who's Calum?' she asked.

I didn't reply. Instead, I looked down at the

business card she'd given me.

"STEVE JONES" it said, but nothing else. From what I could see, there wasn't even a phone number. Instead, all I could see was a black circle on the right hand side that looked like a button.

'Mrs Graham told me how this boy has been causing some trouble,' Mum continued, 'Calum, I mean.'

'He's just hard work, that's all,' I said.

'Mrs Graham also said you've struggled with school at times,' Mum said. 'But that you're beginning to make some friends now.'

'I miss our old life a bit.'

'I know, that's what I told her,' Mum said. 'I'm sorry things haven't been the same since your dad forced us out of our home, but we're over the worst of it now, I'm sure of it,' Mum continued. 'Everything will be all right, you'll see.'

Mum moved forward and enclosed my hands into hers. She pulled me into her soft, yellow jumper and held me so tightly I could barely breathe.

CHAPTER 17

Saturday morning and I felt the urge to build. Maybe it was an attempt to do something, anything to help me to forget what happened that day when Dad came home shouting, and told Mum, Luchia and me that we had to leave and never come back. I also hoped it would take my mind off Level 4 and the possibility of being stuck in the game forever.

I pulled the plastic box from beside the sofa and delved my hands into the colourful mass of building blocks. After throwing some onto the carpet, I looked at the ship I'd built and the castle hoping for some inspiration. In the end, I decided on a house and started with the base. A row of blocks grew into the walls of a room. One room became two, then three and before long the house had transformed into the first floor of a mansion.

'How about a fireplace?' Archie suggested.

'Why not,' I replied, and added a secret panel next to the fireplace. Oh, and a hidden cellar too.

'Haven't you forgotten something?' Archie asked.

I didn't know what he meant at first, but soon realised. Next to the fireplace, I built a small round table.

'Any good?' I asked.

'Perfect,' he replied.

To be honest, it was just what I needed. In fact, I was so engrossed in adding fireplaces, cellars, secret hatches and passageways that I didn't even notice that Archie wasn't with me anymore. Not until he started shouting in my ear that is.

'It's time!' he said.

I didn't know whether to feel scared or excited. In fact, I probably felt a mixture of the two. I looked at the four colours in the room—red, orange, white and green. I tried to take it all in, just in case I was forced to leave the place I called home for a second time.

'Don't forget the life monitors,' Archie said and I grabbed them from the charger.

Next to the charger was the mansion and after pointing my life monitor towards it, I pressed the blue reducer button. I didn't get the chance to see if it had worked because moments later the room started to spin faster and faster until it fell into darkness. The next time I opened my eyes, we were in a field with the forest behind us and the mountains in the distance.

Sir Percival was there too. He was sitting on his white horse beside a single line of wooden planks.

'And so the peasants return to their personal crusade, how wonderful,' he said, 'and a particular welcome back to Chloe.'

'Thank you,' she said.

'I hope you have chosen the correct path this time,' the knight said.

'Me too,' Chloe replied.

'Now, apologies for the delay,' Sir Percival continued. 'You have proven to be such excellent players, we wanted to offer you a proper challenge for Level 4.'

'Not an easy one like before then,' Archie said.

The knight turned to face him. 'I sense a hint of sarcasm. You must remember that if the game was too easy, then just about any peasant or squire would get through to Level 7 and we wouldn't want that, would we?'

'I suppose not,' Archie replied. 'Is there anything you can tell us before we start?'

'Not much I'm afraid,' Sir Percival answered. 'Let's just say that things may not be quite as they seem.'

'Can't you even give us a clue?' Chloe asked.

The knight rubbed at the wispy beard on his chin. 'Well, we will be far stricter on the timing side, so keep an eye on your monitor,' he said. 'It also rains a bit around here, so I hope you've brought a proper hat.'

'This is all really interesting, but how will we know when we've completed the level?' Archie asked.

Sir Percival started to laugh. It began as a bit of a chuckle, but then grew into a loud, grating rasp of a laugh that stopped in an instant.

'As I said before,' he said. 'You will know when the challenge of Level 4 is complete, because I will tell you.'

Almost as soon as he'd finished speaking, he kicked his stirrups and Galahad started to trotted away into the trees. Just as he'd predicted, it started to rain.

'Has anyone got an umbrella?' asked Archie.

'I didn't think we needed them,' I said, as a flash of lightning lit up the top of the mountain in the distance. It was followed by a crash of thunder that shook the ground.

'This way,' shouted Luchia, pointing to the entrance of a cave.

We ran across the field, the rain increasing with every step. By the time we'd reached the mouth-shaped entrance, my shoes and socks were soaking wet.

'Let's get inside,' Archie said. 'If anyone sees anything strange, they need to shout a warning, okay?'

I opened my soaking wet rucksack. 'This might help,' I said, pulling out my second and final glow stick.

'We'll follow you then,' said Luchia.

With me at the front, we headed into the dark tunnel of rock that soon became a downward staircase. The further we descended, the colder it became and, after a while, I began to hear a strange rattling noise. I stopped and stared into the darkness. Then I realised the noise was coming from behind me.

'Is that your teeth?' I asked.

'Yes,' said Chloe, 'I'm freezing.'

'We need to warm up,' said Archie.

The staircase came to an end and opened into a tunnel that headed left and right. Almost directly opposite was a small chamber.

'This looks like as good a place as any,' I said.

Luchia lifted some twigs from her pocket. 'These are too wet. They'll never burn.'

'What about these?' asked Chloe, picking up some wood from the corner of the chamber.

'That's a bit lucky,' Archie said, as he started to arrange the wood into a pile.

'We need to eat something too,' said Luchia, looking at the screen of her life monitor. 'I've only got three and a half bars left.'

I stepped back, almost stumbling over something soft on the floor. I turned and picked it up. 'I've found some bread if that's any good?'

'Almost too good to be true,' said Archie. 'How are we doing for time?'

Luchia looked at her monitor. 'It says eight hours on mine.'

I'd been so nervous about Level 4 but, apart from the storm, it had been easy enough so far. The sesame bread didn't take long to toast. It was really tasty. As we sat, chatted and listened to each other, I almost completely forgot where we were.

'That's a big yawn,' said Luchia.

'Sorry,' I replied, as a wave of sleepiness swept over me.

I looked over at Chloe.

'Wow, I'm really tired,' she said, as she stretched her arms as wide as they would go.

'If anyone needs a sleep, I'll stay awake and keep watch,' Archie offered, as he opened his mouth wide and let out a huge, bear-like yawn.

I was so shattered that even though the floor of the cave was cold and made of stone, it looked really welcoming. I lay down and rested my head on my arm. It didn't take long for sleep to take me away and before I'd had the chance to think about anything else, I'd drifted into dreams.

When I woke up, it was the turn of my teeth to rattle with cold. The fire had almost gone out too, the flames reduced to a few glowing red embers. Then I heard a loud snore, so I picked up my glow stick and waved it around the room to see that everybody was fast asleep.

'Wake up!' I shouted, shaking them all one by one. 'Wake up!'

Eventually, Luchia opened her eyes. 'Let me sleep,' she said, turning over onto her side, 'go away and let me sleep.'

'Archie,' I said, 'come on.'

'What happened?' he asked, between yawns.

'I can't wake anybody up,' I said.

Archie started to stir. 'I think they've tricked us,' he whispered, as he pushed himself up to kneeling.

'Maybe it was something in the food,' I said, remembering Sir Percival's words. 'Things may not be quite as they seem' he'd warned us. Yet, when the storm came, we ran to the nearest, convenient cave. When we wanted to start a fire, Chloe just happened to find some dry wood. Then, of course, a loaf of bread appeared from nowhere.

The sound of the swirling swish of the sea confirmed my worst fears.

'Ah oh,' said Luchia, as she sat up, pointing into the gloom of the tunnel.

'Long tentacles, white bodies, green eyes,' I said. 'Is that what I think it is?'

'And this way too,' said Chloe, pointing in the other direction where a group of seaspirits had gathered by the staircase to block any hope of escape.

CHAPTER 18

I pointed my glow stick one way then the other. For a moment, I wondered why the shimmering spirits weren't moving particularly quickly. Then I realised— they had us exactly where they wanted.

'There's something else,' said Luchia, looking at her monitor. 'We've only got twenty-five minutes left.'

'You don't think Sir Percival will decide we've done enough then?' I asked.

'Hardly,' she replied.

'It doesn't have to be all of us,' said Archie, taking the glow stick from me and pointing it along the tunnel. 'When I say run, you run okay?'

'No way,' I said. 'It's my fault, because I found the

bread. If anyone's going to get stuck here, it should be me.'

It was Chloe's turn to step forward. 'No, Max, it should be me,' she said.

'That's not fair,' I said. 'You've become such a good friend.'

'Thank you,' she replied. 'I think you're all amazing too and I really appreciate it.'

'But it's still not fair,' Luchia said.

'It is,' said Chloe. 'Because I'm the only one the "getting stuck in the game" thing doesn't apply to.'

I looked at Luchia, then back at Chloe. 'Are you sure?'

'Certain,' Chloe said, taking the glow stick from Archie.

'But have you seen how many there are?' I asked. 'You might have a panic attack.'

'I've thought about that,' Chloe said. 'I still want to try.'

Archie turned to Luchia and me. 'If Chloe is going to do what I think she is, we need to lie on the floor.'

'He's right,' said Chloe. 'Stay down for as long as you can.'

Reluctantly, I did as she said.

Glow stick in one hand, Chloe used her other hand to edge along the cold stone walls. She hadn't gone very far when she stopped—the terror on her face suggesting she was about to go into panic mode. Then she closed her eyes and took a deep breath. Moments later, she held the glow stick high above her shoulders and waved it from left to right.

'We've found one…let us take her with us…into

the deep,' the spirits whispered as Chloe turned and ran.

From where I was, I could just about see a cloud of spectral shapes with dangling tentacles, chasing her along the tunnel.

'Let me have her...I want her...she's mine,' whispered one of the spirits as it raced overhead.

I tried not to think about what was happening, but then I heard a short, high-pitched scream as they engulfed poor Chloe in a cloud of white.

'We've got to go!' I picked myself up from the floor. 'They'll soon realise what's happened.'

'What about Chloe?' Luchia said.

'Sorry, Luchia, but Max is right,' said Archie. 'Otherwise she'll have sacrificed herself for nothing.'

My eyes adapting to the darkness, I ran up the

staircase in the hope I'd be able to find the tunnel that led to the exit. When I reached the top, however, the tunnel had split into two passageways.

'Which one?' Archie asked.

'Right,' I said, hopefully.

I stopped at the sound of metal scraping against the stone walls. The beating of wings followed, accompanied by screaming and shouting.

'Catch them!'

'Chop them!'

'Feast on them!'

'Turn around!' I shouted.

'Make your mind up,' Archie said, as we headed along the second passageway, with the vampire berserkers in pursuit.

I looked up to see a mouth-shaped light at the end of the tunnel.

'Don't forget to pick up the swords,' I cried as we raced through the exit and into the sunshine.

As soon as we were outside, we stopped, turned and waited for the vampires. I lifted my hands to shield my eyes from the expected flash as they exploded from their exposure to the sun. Unfortunately, nothing happened. Instead of bursting into flames, the vampires streamed out of the exit and into the sky above us.

'They're wearing clothes,' said Archie.

'Cloaks,' I replied, as I looked a bit closer. 'Protective cloaks to shield them from the light.'

Luchia ran over. 'Don't give up now,' she shouted, as the berserkers flew towards us, their eyes bulging from their contorted faces.

'Come on, Archie,' I said, and together, we followed Luchia onto a row of wooden planks that headed across the field and away from the caves. Either side of the planks was a green carpet of moss, with the occasional tall, narrow reed poking its way through.

'Oh excellent,' said Archie. 'A swamp.'

'Stay on the boards and we'll be okay,' Luchia replied.

We'd only gone a few paces, when we heard another noise.

Thump…Thump, then again, but this time even louder.

'Giant,' Archie said, between breaths, 'fifty-metre-high, man-eating mountain giant on his way.'

We jumped from one wooden plank to the next, the repeated cries of vampires becoming louder by the second.

I tried not to look but Luchia turned around. This is probably why she lost her footing as she skidded, tripped and toppled into the swamp.

Squelch!

By the time I reached her, she was already up to her waist in mud, her hands stretching upwards.

'Grab hold of her wrist, Archie,' I said. 'Luchia, stop waving your arms around!'

Seconds later, Luchia's terrified face disappeared below the surface of the pungent smelling mud. I glanced at Archie and then, with a heave, we pulled her upwards.

'Help!' she cried, her head poking through the surface.

'Nearly there,' I said, but just as she rose, the suction of the swamp dragged her back down again.

'One more go, Max,' shouted Archie. 'Come on!'

I tightened my grip around her wrist and pulled as hard as I could. Slowly she rose, then a bit more until finally, with a loud pop, Luchia was free.

Her face covered in patches of mud, she lay beside us on the wooden plank. 'I thought I'd never get out,' she said between gasps.

'No time for chatting I'm afraid,' said Archie, checking his life monitor. 'We've only got three and a half minutes left.'

He'd barely finished his sentence when a menacing shadow crept along the ground beside us. I looked up to a vampire berserker diving towards us.

'I've caught them.'

'Now chop them.'

'Feast on them.'

'I'm sorry, you two,' said Archie. 'But this is the end.'

'One last chance,' I said, as I pulled the life monitor from my pocket and pressed the expander button. Nothing. I pressed it again, harder this time and then, as if from nowhere, a pathway of stepping stones lifted itself from the centre of the swamp. I looked again to see that something else had started to rise through the mud. What started as a small house soon grew into something much bigger. It was the first floor of a half-built mansion.

'Come on,' I said, as we ran towards the doorway. Not that we were safe, not yet. Accompanied by a rattle of chainmail, and with their swords pointing towards us, the berserkers flew in through the open windows and down through the ceiling.

'Head for the fireplace,' I shouted as I ran past the round table and lifted the wooden board next to the grate. 'This way!' I said.

Down the concrete steps we went and I let go of the cellar hatch that closed behind us with a thud. My breath shallow and quick, my heart racing, I rested my back against the cold stone wall. As my eyes adjusted to the gloom, I noticed a shimmering breastplate that moved forward out of the shadows.

'I knew you'd come,' said the knight, smiling. 'For a bunch of nobodies, you have shown remarkable resilience once again, and for this, I salute you.'

Archie climbed back up the first few steps of the stone staircase. His hands grabbed at the metal handle on the cellar hatch so tightly, it was as though he'd never let go.

'Don't worry,' Sir Percival said. 'You are safe from the enemy in here.'

'But what if the giant turns up, he'd smash the place to pieces wouldn't he?'

'You're probably right,' said the knight. 'He'd smash anything to pieces given the chance, but there's no need to worry about him, not until the next level anyway.'

Luchia stepped forward. 'Are you saying what I

think you're saying?'

'That depends,' Sir Percival replied.

'We've made it past Level 4 haven't we?' I asked.

Sir Percival nodded. 'Just three more levels to go and your entire quest will be at an end.'

'Not long to go then,' said Luchia. 'Wow!'

'Believe me, you've barely even started,' the knight replied. 'You must remember that with every challenge, the stakes increase and there are still a few surprises to come.'

I started to laugh, I don't know why. It might have been the excitement, maybe it was relief, but whatever it was, I couldn't stop myself.

'You look a little muddy, Luchia,' said the knight. 'How was the swamp?'

'Cold,' she replied, 'and a bit stinky.'

'Fortunately, your very own Lancelot was on hand to save you,' Sir Percival said, and then turned towards me. 'Talking of which, it was an ingenious use of the expander button, Max. We think it's within the rules, but we'll let you know.'

'Did you see the table upstairs?' I asked.

'Yes, it is most perfectly round' he replied, 'and I look forward to using it.'

'What about Chloe?' asked Luchia. 'Is she safe?'

'The damsel in distress you mean?' said the knight. 'The good news is, and as you have correctly worked out, she isn't locked in the game.'

'And the bad news?'

'Oh that,' said the knight. 'Well, to continue playing, she'd need to start from the very beginning.'

'She could catch us up then?' Luchia said. 'Maybe?'

Sir Percival rubbed his chin. 'It would be extremely difficult.'

'But possible?' I asked.

'Improbable,' he replied.

We didn't say anything else because we didn't get the chance. Even in the gloom of the cellar, I could see the pair of yellow butterflies that fluttered past. This, of course, meant only one thing.

I always have a mixture of feelings when I get home. It's great to get past a level and I do feel a massive sense of satisfaction when we do. Most of the time, however, being at home is just a little bit dull.

The good news this time was that Mum seemed different. Instead of some of the niggling comments like 'why haven't you cleaned your room' or 'take your muddy shoes off when you come into the house', she started asking me questions about school and about life.

She wasn't the only one to have changed.

'Good morning, Max,' Calum said, when I went back to school. Then he smiled, even if it did look a bit lopsided.

'Is Anuska with him?' I asked Archie.

'Yes,' he replied.

'Acting strange?'

'Definitely. Almost pleasant.'

Apart from that, the others in my class continued to talk to me, especially Matt Bellow, even if I did have to cover my ears when he spoke. I also noticed that for the first time since we'd started the school year Chloe wasn't on her own anymore. In fact, every time I saw her, she seemed to be sitting and chatting with the other girls in our class.

'What you did was amazing,' I said, when I spoke to her at break time. 'I hope the seaspirits didn't hurt you.'

'It was a bit scary,' she replied. 'But then I thought about how Luchia had told me to keep calm and take deep breaths when that fire alarm made me panic. The next thing I knew, I was back at home.'

'They didn't hurt you then.'

'Just these,' she said, showing me her arm and a few puffy white circles. 'They're a bit like nettle stings.'

She rolled down her sleeve to cover them up.

'The knight said you'd have to start from the beginning if you wanted to catch us.'

'I thought that might happen,' she said. 'It's okay though.'

'Are you sure?'

'It's weird. But ever since I started playing Ma-Chia, I've felt more confident about things.'

'I think I know what you mean.'

'Seriously, Max, it's made a massive difference. I'm so grateful to you and the others for letting me join in.'

'We're grateful to you too,' I said. 'You were really brave.'

'Thank you.'

I didn't say anymore. Although Chloe looked happy, her eyes turned red and filled with water as though she was about to cry.

'How was your day?' Mum asked, when I got home. Before I could answer, she took hold of my hand. I went into the kitchen to see Luchia was sitting on one of the tall breakfast stools next to the table.

'Hello, Max,' Luchia said. 'Is there much going on at school?'

'It's eventful,' I replied.

Just then, the phone rang. 'I'll get it,' Mum said and left us alone in the kitchen.

'I can't believe it,' I said. 'You look so much better.'

'I feel it too.'

I sat on the stool beside her. 'I was speaking to Chloe today.'

'How is she?'

'She's fine,' I said. 'In fact, she's better than fine and says it's all down to Ma-Chia. She even thanked me.'

'You should be proud of yourselves,' said Archie. 'This game you've created is incredible.'

'Archie's right,' Luchia said. 'When I was in that swamp, it was awful. I thought I was going to drown.'

'We would never have allowed that to happen,' said Archie.

'Thank you,' she said. 'But ever since you pulled me out of the mud, my temperature has gone down and the itchiness has disappeared.'

'Does this mean you'll be coming into school soon?' I asked.

'It shouldn't be long, maybe a week.'

'Fantastic!'

What a day. I turned up the radio and as the music played I started to dance around the kitchen. Luchia joined in too and I'm sure Archie would have done if he could.

It didn't last long though.

I don't seem to be allowed happiness for more than a few moments. As a cold wind wrapped itself around me, I started to slow down. I closed my eyes and of course she was there. Anuska started to dance with me at first—her grey, snake-like figure mocking my every move as she swayed from side to side.

'Max, are you okay?' Luchia said, but then I fell off the stool and onto the floor.

'She's back,' I said, tightening my hands around my chest in an effort to keep warm.

'Max,' Luchia said, as she knelt beside me. 'You look terrible.'

I forced my eyes open. I tried to resist closing them again, but I couldn't. It was as though I simply couldn't stop myself from checking if she was still there.

'Think of something else, Max,' said Archie. 'Use that imagination of yours and fight her off.'

I did as Archie said. Unfortunately, all I could think about was Ma-Chia. My mind became full of the castle, the forest, the mountains and then, a pit full of snakes.

'Thank you,' said Anuska, as her image started to fade. 'We look forward to seeing you soon.'

'Are you all right, Max?' asked Luchia.

'That was horrible,' I said. 'Where did she come from?'

'Clever spirit,' Archie said. 'Catching us when we're off guard.'

Once I'd started to breathe properly again, Luchia helped me up and I slumped down on the stool.

'Archie,' I said. 'If we wanted to leave the game, I

suppose we could, couldn't we?'

'What do you mean?' he asked.

'Now everything seems to be okay again,' I said. 'It doesn't seem right to risk everything, just to get past a few levels.'

'But we have to finish it now don't we?' Luchia asked. 'That's right isn't it, Archie?'

We looked at him. I think we were both hoping that he'd say something clever and wise.

'If we decided not to carry on, we'd effectively lose,' Archie said, 'and both Calum and Anuska would have us exactly where they wanted.'

The door to the kitchen opened.

'Goodness me, you two look gloomy,' Mum said. 'I'll make some tea shall I? That should cheer you up.'

CHAPTER 20

'We'll do the washing up, Mum,' Luchia said, when we'd finished eating. 'Won't we, Max?'

I nodded.

Mum walked to the kitchen door. 'Thanks. I'll leave you to it.'

'She's so massively over-protective at the moment,' Luchia said, 'she'd have only sent me to my room if I hadn't offered.'

I turned on the tap and squeezed some washing up liquid into the sink. 'It's fine.'

'Are you sure you're all right?' Luchia asked.

'Yes.'

'Does she attack you often? Anuska I mean.'

'Now and again,' I said, as I watched the sink fill up with white, frothy bubbles. 'Just think, this might even be the last time we ever do this.'

Luchia leant past me and plunged her hand into the washing up bowl. She picked up a handful of bubbles and threw them in my direction.

'Cheer up!' she said.

As soon as we'd finished putting the plates and cutlery away, we headed to the back room.

'I haven't been in here for ages,' Luchia said. 'I'd almost forgotten about the different colours on the walls.'

I grabbed my plastic box. 'Do you recognise this?' I said, showing her the mansion I'd built.

'Is this where we hid in the last level?' she asked.

'Yep.'

'So that's what Sir Percival was talking about when he mentioned the expander button,' she added.

'Pretty good idea eh?' said Archie.

'I might have an even better one,' Luchia replied, picking up a few building blocks and handing them to me. 'Do you think you could make a dragon?'

'I could have a go,' I replied, and started with a long thin piece that narrowed at one end.

'What's that supposed to be?' Luchia asked, sniggering.

'The tail,' I replied, 'what do you think?'

I didn't wait for a reply but added the body, the wings and a head that included a pair of beady-looking eyes. I was quite pleased with it.

'It looks more like an eagle than a dragon,' Luchia said.

'Thanks,' I said. 'It wasn't my idea to build it.'

I was about to take it apart and have another go, when I noticed the room had started to darken and then spin.

'It's time,' said Archie. 'Good luck, everyone.'

When I opened my eyes, we'd been transported into a world of white cloud that circled around us.

'Wow, that's incredible,' said Luchia, as the cloud began to separate.

She was right. I've only been on a few mountains but they were fairly small ones I suppose. This one was huge and so high it almost felt as though we were flying.

'Hello there, my peasant friends,' said the knight, standing beside his white horse, Galahad, whose tail flicked in the sunlight, 'and welcome to Dead Mountain.'

'Dead Mountain?' Luchia asked.

'There is nothing here, except for the rocks and the earth,' Sir Percival said.

'Lovely name,' said Archie. 'Most appealing.'

As the cloud continued to drift away, I could see a stream that twisted along the valley below us. My eyes followed the stream towards the castle in the distance, a distance that seemed incredibly far away.

'That is your quest, your holy grail if you like,' Sir Percival said, as he mounted his horse. 'All you have to do is make it to the castle and you will have completed Level 5.'

'All we have to do?' asked Archie, sardonically.

'What's the matter now?' Sir Percival asked. 'You requested a target and we have provided one.'

Archie stepped to the edge of the mountain. 'But it's miles away.'

'And don't forget, the enemy of time is also against you,' said the knight. 'Tick tock, tick tock.'

Galahad trotted away and headed along a path that weaved its way through a cluster of rocks.

'I think we should follow him,' said Archie. 'At least until we get attacked by whatever it is they're going to attack us with first.'

'You're such an optimist,' Luchia said.

'Realist,' he suggested.

The track was wide enough for us to walk beside each other at the top. As we started to descend, however, the path narrowed and curved around the edge of the mountain.

'Watch out!' shouted Luchia.

I only glanced, but that was enough to see a pair of dragons above our heads. Before any of us had the chance to react, the first of them released a ball of fire that raced in our direction. Within moments, it crashed into the mountainside above us, its flames dispersing amongst the surrounding rocks.

I almost tripped over but somehow managed to keep my balance as another ball of fire was sent from the dragon's mouth. This time it wasn't aimed above our heads and was heading straight at us. I threw myself from the path. Head first, feet first, then into a somersault, I bounced and bumped down the slope until I came to a stop on a small, flat ridge.

'Ow!' I said, as I sat up and brushed away a mixture of blood and dirt from my elbow. I then looked for the others, but unfortunately, they were nowhere to be seen.

I started to panic as a breath of cold slipped through my clothes and onto my chest. I closed my eyes and there she was, her grey body swaying from side to side. Shivering, I hid behind a rock and glanced past to confirm my worst fears. Somehow, Anuska and Calum were not only back in the game, they were now only twenty metres away.

A dark shadow swept along the ground beside me and I looked up to see a dragon flying towards them. As it came closer, the beating of its huge wings created swirls of air like a helicopter coming in to land. I was about to shout a warning when I realised that things didn't seem quite right. Instead of attacking him with fireballs, the dragon hovered above Calum.

'I saw one of them over there,' he said to the dragon and then pointed towards me.

I dived to the ground. As the dragon angled its huge wings in my direction, I crawled to the edge of the ridge to see a drop of about a hundred metres. It was risky, but I had no choice other than to jump and hope. I was just about to close my eyes and go when a different dragon appeared, at least, it could have been a dragon. If I'm honest, it looked a bit like an eagle.

Then I heard a voice I recognised.

'Max, get on!'

The odd-shaped dragon tilted its head to one side and there she was, Luchia, flying on its back. Archie was there too, so I grabbed hold of his outstretched hand as he pulled me on board.

'Should I recognise this?' I asked.

'Yes,' Luchia replied. 'I decided to bring it after all.'

'But it looks a bit like an eagle,' I said.

'Told you,' Luchia said. 'I think we should call it a dreagle.'

I'd only been on its back for a moment when a fireball raced towards us.

'Hang on!' Archie said, as the dreagle twisted in mid-flight, hurtled upwards and swooped into a dive.

'That was close,' I said, as the fireball whizzed past.

I looked to the left, where Calum was riding on the back of one of the dragons. I looked to the right, to see another dragon and, this time, Anuska had wrapped herself around its neck.

'I think I'm going to be sick,' said Archie, as the dreagle turned, swooped and twisted to avoid another fireball.

Thump…Thump.

'Don't look now,' said Luchia, but, of course, all of us did.

'Oh, that's just great,' said Archie.

It wasn't only dragons that were chasing us. Behind them, and gaining with every step, was a striding, bounding, fifty-metre-high man-eating mountain giant.

'Watch out!' I cried, as a huge grey fist came bursting through the sky. In response, the dreagle flew into a final somersault and then, with one last dive, she flew towards the turrets of the castle below.

CHAPTER 21

The dreagle didn't even land but just hovered above the stone floor at the top of the castle tower.

'Come on,' Sir Percival said, helping us down from her back.

I wanted to say thank you to the dreagle, but by the time I'd turned around, she'd already set off into the sky. The giant, meanwhile, stood about ten metres away with his grey fists raised and his dark eyes staring.

'Don't tempt him,' said the knight, who urged us through a wooden door that he bolted behind us.

As soon as we were inside the tower, Archie started shaking his hand. 'Thank you for everything,' he said.

143

'We wouldn't have made it without you.'

Sir Percival looked at Archie. 'You have shown much bravery in completing Level 5,' he said. 'Nevertheless, there are still two levels to go.'

Archie let go of his hand. 'You're joking. I thought that was it.'

'Of course not,' Sir Percival replied.

'Do we go home then?' I asked. 'Between levels I mean.'

'Not this time I'm afraid,' said the knight. 'By the way, from whence did you acquire that strange-looking bird?'

'I made it,' I said.

'I reduced it,' said Luchia.

'And then she expanded it,' Archie added.

'A bit like the mansion then?' Sir Percival said. 'You made it in your other world and then you brought it into mine.'

'Yes,' I said. 'Is that okay?'

The knight rubbed at the wispy beard on his chin in the same way he always seems to do when making a decision.

'Once again you have stretched the parameters of the code of conduct,' he replied after a while. 'However, as both of the items were manufactured by yourselves, I can confirm this is acceptable.'

'Phew,' I said.

'Okay, it is time for me to wish you good fortune,' Sir Percival said, 'and for you to prove yourselves worthy of the prize.'

He turned and, with a clattering of metal boots on stone floor, he disappeared down the spiralling staircase in the corner of the room.

'Now what?' Luchia asked.

'Well, I suppose we follow Max,' said Archie. 'After all, he built the castle.'

'Not all of it,' I said. 'Anyway, it's been changed so much.'

'Archie's right though,' Luchia added. 'You must have some idea.'

No pressure then.

From where we were, there was only one way to go and I headed towards the staircase. At least I remembered building this bit. After we'd twisted and turned our way down, the stairs opened out into a larger corridor. In the corridor were two wooden doors, side by side.

I remembered building these as well. Not that I had any idea what was on the other side.

'Go for lucky left,' Archie said.

Luchia stepped forward. 'It might be important. Surely we can think of something better than lucky left.'

I shrugged and opened the left-hand door.

'Hello, Max, I'm so pleased to see you,' said Calum, 'and so are the rest of us.'

He pointed upward at the 'us', who turned out to be a group of cloak-wearing, vampire berserkers that were hanging from the ceiling.

'Catch them.'

'Chop them.'

 I slammed the door closed, but then a familiar cold shiver ran through me. I turned around to see the grey figure of Anuska blocking the staircase at the end of the corridor.

Beside her, were a group of snakes that slithered towards us.

'Hello, Max,' she said. 'Thank you for bringing my children into the game.'

Luchia quickly opened the second wooden door on the right. 'This way,' she said.

The door closed behind us with a bang and I twisted the iron key to lock us in.

'Why does it always have to be snakes?' said Archie.

'It was Anuska's fault,' I replied. 'She forced me to think about them when we were in the kitchen.'

'Oh well,' said Luchia. 'At least the seaspirits seem to have disappeared.'

Archie started pacing across the wooden floor. 'Let me get this straight,' he said. 'Both the jesters and the seaspirits have gone. In their place, we now have to deal with dragons and the things that terrify me the most.'

'And the crazy berserking vampires,' Luchia said.

'And a mountain giant,' I added, as I looked through the small square window to see the biggest, meanest looking black eyes staring back.

'I think he wants to come in,' Luchia said. 'Any ideas anybody?'

'Maybe there's a secret passageway,' I replied. 'You know how these things work sometimes.'

'If there is I bet it will lead to a dungeon,' said Luchia.

'Yes,' Archie said, 'and no doubt the dungeon will be filled with dragons.'

I looked at them both, one then the other. 'Dungeons and dragons?' I said. 'Are you sure we're in the right game?'

'Very funny,' Luchia said.

I moved to the edge of the room, my fingers searching the cold stones on the wall. 'How much time have we got?' I asked.

'I hoped you wouldn't ask,' Archie replied. 'If I'm reading this monitor correctly, we have about twenty minutes.'

We all looked at one another.

'That's why they've trapped us in here,' I said.

Archie started to pace around the room. 'I've been thinking,' he said.

'That's dangerous,' Luchia said.

'No, seriously,' Archie continued, as he moved towards the wooden door. 'I've been thinking how well you two seem to be doing.'

'Thanks,' I said, as I continued to search every part of the room I could reach.

'It's my turn to face my biggest fear,' he said.

Before I'd had the chance to react, he'd turned the key in the lock.

'No!' Luchia shouted.

By the time I reached the door, Archie was already being chased by Calum, the snakes and the vampire berserkers.

'Catch him.'

'Chop him.'

'Feast on him,' they cried.

'They've got Archie,' I said. 'What are we going to do?'

'The thing he wanted us to do,' Luchia replied. 'Finish the game. Come on.'

I looked along the corridor one last time. As I did so, some of the vampires turned and flew in our direction.

'This way,' Luchia shouted.

We ran down the spiralling staircase, the shouts and threats from vampires getting louder by the moment. At the bottom of the stairs was an opening onto a wooden ledge that ran along the wall of the castle. We'd only run a few steps when a set of grey knuckles smashed through the wall, the force of the giant's fist scattering stone and rubble to the castle floor.

'Keep going, Max,' Luchia said.

'Look!' I said, pointing to the courtyard below

where Sir Percival was standing with his hands behind his back.

A booming growl followed, as a second fist smashed its way through the castle wall. This time, it was in front of us.

'Game over!' I heard Calum shout, as the wall collapsed and the wooden ledge disappeared from beneath our feet.

I threw out my arms to grab onto something, anything to stop me from falling but it was no good. Air whistling past me, I tensed my body. Instead of the crash landing I was expecting, however, I fell onto the scale-covered back of a dragon. Luchia landed beside me and, as I sat up, I realised that the dragon we'd fallen onto looked a bit like an eagle.

'Woohoo!' I shouted, but then I looked up.

In front of us, the mountain giant stood with his hands open. His fingers were pointing outwards as though he was getting ready to crush us into dust. He didn't get the chance as the dreagle flew upwards, sideways and through his despairing grasp. One more turn, one more corkscrew swoop and a tumble through the rushing air and she landed in the middle of the courtyard. Her breath panting, her chest heaving, the huge bird lowered her back and we slid along her tail onto the ground.

'Thank you,' Luchia said to the dreagle, hugging her around the neck.

'Thank you from me too,' I said, as, with a powerful beat of her wings, she lifted herself into the sky and soared over what was left of the castle walls.

I looked at Luchia and smiled a smile so wide I

almost hurt myself.

'Impressive, very impressive indeed,' Sir Percival said, walking towards us. 'Now, I just need to check your monitors.'

I handed mine over and Luchia did the same.

He looked at the screens, then back at us.

'This is a terrible shame,' he said. 'A terrible, terrible shame.'

'What is?' I asked.

'That your quest is almost complete,' the knight said, handing the monitors back to us. 'Max and Luchia, you have shown powers of incredible fortitude to get this far.'

'Thank you,' I said. 'But what about Archie, we wouldn't have made it without him.'

'Ah, yes, your friend,' Sir Percival said. 'Forget about him because you now have the opportunity to attempt Level 7 and win the castle for yourselves.'

I looked at Luchia again.

'But what about Archie?' she said. 'Is he okay?'

'Oh, I see, the castle is not enough,' the knight replied. He looked at the giant, who towered above us. 'If I'm honest, there should have been more of it left, but someone got a bit busy with his fists.'

The giant shrugged.

'I tell you what, if you succeed, I will also offer you the powers to transport yourselves to the island,' Sir Percival continued. 'In which case, you won't even need Archie.'

'It's not about whether we need him or not,' Luchia said.

'But there's a game to complete. Level 7 is within

your grasp.'

'You're not listening,' I said. 'Our friends are more important than any game.'

At this point, Calum ran over. Anuska was beside him, accompanied by a slithering nest of snakes. 'If they're too scared, we don't mind having a go,' he said.

'Well, this is an interesting development,' Sir Percival said. 'What do you think, Max and Luchia? I suggest you consider your decision very, very carefully.'

'What should we do?' I asked Luchia.

'Isn't it obvious?'

I stepped towards the knight. 'Thank you for the offer, but we'd rather have Archie back.'

'And Chloe,' Luchia added. 'Because she helped us too.'

Sir Percival gave us one of those stern looks people give you when they think you've done something wrong.

'Are you absolutely sure?' he said. 'You've done so well to get this far.'

'Yes,' we said in unison.

'Fools,' said Calum. 'We win, just like I told you we

would.'

Anuska slithered beside him. 'And you lose,' she said.

Sir Percival wandered around the courtyard with his back to us, his metal boots kicking at the dirt and stones.

'Come on,' Calum said. 'The sooner we start, the sooner we get to keep the prize.'

'I already have a special place in mind for Archie,' Anuska hissed, glancing at the circle of snakes that slid beside her. 'With my little children in the deepest pit I can find.'

'Yea,' said Calum. 'We might even force you to stay for a while, Max. You too, Luchia.'

He'd barely finished speaking, when the ground shook and a crack opened up beside us. As the crevice widened, a golden bridge lifted and stretched from the earth as it extended upwards into the clouds. An enormous brown bird appeared in the distance. As it approached us, it became so huge it seemed to block out the entire sky.

'Griffon vulture,' Sir Percival said. 'A magnificent specimen.'

'We'll tell you all about it,' said Calum, as the vulture soared over the bridge. 'Maybe.'

Calum stepped forward. Anuska slithered alongside.

The knight turned. 'Not so fast my selfish young friends,' he said. 'Level 7 is a different kind of test.'

'Just tell us what we need to do and we'll do it,' Calum said.

'You have already done enough,' Sir Percival

replied. 'You see, Level 7 was a test of honour and loyalty.'

'Well that's definitely us then,' Calum said. 'Without our help, the ending to the game would have been really boring.'

'You have helped yourselves,' said the knight. 'Do you remember what I said when Anuska begged me for another chance?'

Calum opened his arms in protest. 'That we needed to play the game in the right way and we have.'

'And yet, at the end, all you can think about is yourselves,' the knight said. 'Exactly the opposite of what Ma-Chia is all about.'

Calum's shoulders tightened and lowered, his expression hardening into a snarl. Anuska coiled herself beside him and pointed her head as though she was getting ready to strike.

She didn't get the chance.

Instead, Sir Percival clapped his hands and, in a flash, Calum and Anuska had vanished into dust.

'Goodbye,' he said, 'and good riddance.'

As the dust cleared, a different figure strode towards us. He was coloured blue and had the most sparkling, hazel-coloured eyes.

'Archie,' Luchia said. 'You're back!'

'You didn't think I'd leave you for long did you?' he said.

'But what about Chloe?' I asked.

'That could be a little more difficult,' the knight said, pointing at the egg clock on one of our monitors. 'Even if she started the game now, she'd never make it all the way through the levels in time.'

'Unless she had a magic bike,' Archie said.

'That might do it,' Sir Percival confirmed.

Both of them turned and looked at me.

'What?' I said. 'You mean Steve?'

I fumbled in my pockets for the card he gave me. Trouser pocket, shirt pocket, coat pocket, trouser pocket again.

'I can't find it,' I said.

I tried again, each and every pocket for a second and third time until my fingers brushed against a small piece of card. On the right-hand side of the card was a small black circle in the shape of a button.

'Do you think it will work?'

'Why not give it a go?' Archie said.

I pressed the button. Nothing happened for a few seconds, but then the portcullis started to rise, accompanied by the sound of chain scraping against rock. Slowly but surely, the metal door forced its way up through the grooves to reveal a man sitting on a white bike at the bottom of the stone steps.

'Steve,' I said.

At the side of the bike was an extra seat.

'Chloe,' Luchia said.

'Congratulations to you all on completing Level 7,' Sir Percival said. 'Don't worry, you still get to keep your prize. The warning I gave about you losing everything was just my idea of a jolly jape.'

'What happens now?' I asked.

'I thought you might like to show me around,' said Steve, who'd climbed the steps and was now standing beside us. 'I think Chloe wouldn't mind having a proper look too.'

I glanced at the knight, who nodded. 'I think we can allow it,' he said.

'Can I ask you something?' Luchia asked. 'Why do you keep saying "we"?'

'Oh sorry, of course, I've never actually introduced my companions have I,' Sir Percival said. 'The "we" are those who have assisted in constructing the entire kingdom. The seaspirits, the vampire berserkers, the jesters, the dragons, the talking forest and the swamp. Even the giant has helped me to construct the last level or two. Before he smashed up the castle that is.'

'Friends of yours then,' I said.

'Not exactly friends of mine,' the knight replied. 'But characters you and Luchia have created. Sometimes without you even realising.'

'Some of them are a bit strange,' I said.

'Well,' he said. 'Sometimes the realms of our imaginations are a bit strange, aren't they?'

I looked up to see the beating wings of our dreagle as she landed beside us. The two dragons came next, the ones that Calum and Anuska had previously ridden.

'I hope you all enjoy the tour,' said Sir Percival.

The dreagle took off first with Luchia, Chloe and me on its back.

The two dragons followed with Steve and Archie. After the giant had shown us his enormous house at the back of Dead Mountain, we headed towards the caves. Using a set of torches, the vampires and seaspirits gave us a tour of the tunnels. I even had a small look into the abyss in which the jesters were kept. I decided it was better to leave them where they were. The strangest part, though, was having a conversation with the talking forest.

Eventually, we made it back to where we'd started Level 1 at the beginning of the game.

'You've both done really well,' said Archie, as we stood on the beach.

'We've ALL done really well,' I corrected him.

I gazed out across the sea, then turned around and looked at the forest, the mountains and the castle.

'Is this really all ours?' I said.

It all looked so different somehow. Brighter, more colourful and as though the entire kingdom was covered in the brightest, twinkling stars.

'Every last bit of it,' Archie replied.

'Wow!' said Luchia.

I'd only been looking for a moment or two, when a pair of yellow butterflies floated and fluttered past.

It was time to go home.

Although it was great to have finished, I also felt a bit low at first. Then I started to realise how lucky I'd been. Lucky to have been in the right place at the right time to help Steve. Lucky that Archie had come along at just the right time to make such a massive difference in my life.

I'm also lucky to have a sister like Luchia and we've recently spoken about when we should tell Mum about our little secret. In the end, we decided we might leave it a while. As I've said before, the last thing I want to do is worry her about my stuff. She sees a bit of Steve now and they often go dancing and do other things that grown-ups do. I often wonder whether he mentions the game to her. I've asked him not to and he's promised me that he won't.

Archie moved on almost immediately to look after someone else. Apparently, he still has a bit to do before he achieves his redemption. It was sad when he went though, particularly the first day. He told me that he didn't want to leave either. He said how much he'd enjoyed his few weeks with Luchia and me, but that it is simply time for him to carry on with his work.

Most importantly, we still play Ma-Chia. We've chosen a time on Friday night when all of us go back—Luchia, Chloe and me. Archie joins us too when he can and sometimes he forces Calum to come along. Not that Calum is allowed to join in. Instead, he has to watch from outside, which seems like the absolute worst punishment to me.

We're currently on Level 10. The griffon vultures in Level 8 took a bit of getting past and it seemed to take forever to escape the unicorns in Level 9. I just hope that we find a way to make it past the army of centaurs.

There's something else too. It doesn't happen very often, but every now and then I feel cold wind wrap itself around me. If I close my eyes, sometimes she's there and sometimes she's not. Then I remember what Sir Percival said and tell myself that Anuska is just a strange part of my imagination.

So I think for a bit, take a deep breath, and tell her to go away and leave me alone.

Map Of The Game

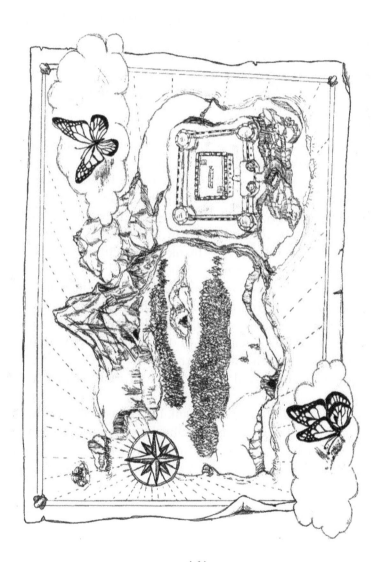

Acknowledgements

I am honoured to be Patron of Reading at Blessed Edward Oldcorne Catholic College in Worcester and I am extremely grateful to all the staff for making me feel so welcome and for Linda Bromyard's amazing assistance. Thank you as well to all the students who read this story and provided me with the most incredible feedback. Also, thank you to those at a number of local schools for allowing me further opportunities to follow my dream.

I'd also like to say thank you to The Bibliobufffers, from the University of Worcester, for their help with the initial development of the story. Having recently completed a degree in Creative Writing & English Literature, I'd like to thank the lecturers, fellow students, Worcester Students' Union, the Communications Department and all the incredible people I've met along the way who have helped me find myself once again. Likewise, I'd like to say thank you to Voices Unlimited whose influence set me on this path, and to Worcester Writers' Circle for their encouragement and advice as I read each chapter to them.

Most of all, I'd like to thank the fantastic illustrator, Seraphim Bryant, who brought the story alive in such an amazing way, my wife for encouraging me to do this and Black Pear Press for their editing suggestions and support in providing a platform to showcase this story.